After failing to save her father's life, Dr. Lise Dawson seeks refuge and renewal in the primitive paradise of Papua New Guinea. She's a doctor who no longer wishes to doctor, and a woman who has found love to be unsafe.

Lise wants nothing to do with coffee plantation owner Simon McDowell, a risk-taker like her father. If Simon is willing to take risks with his life, there's no telling what he'll do with Lise's heart.

Passion of the Drums is a work of fiction.
Names, characters and incidents are products of the
author's imagination and are not to be construed as real.
Any resemblance to actual events or locales
or persons, living or dead, is entirely coincidental.

Published 2000 by
The Fiction Works
Omaha • Lake Tahoe
www.fictionworks.com

Copyright © 1999
by Gael Morrison

All rights reserved. No part of this book may be
reproduced or transmitted in any form or by any
electronic or mechanical means, including photocopying,
recording or by any information storage and retrieval
system, without the written permission of the
Publisher, except where permitted by law.

ISBN 1-58124-659-5

Printed in the
United States of America

To Alice,
Wishing you love, magic & the spirit of adventure!
♡ Gael Morrison

Passion of the Drums

Gael Morrison

For Ron,

with Love, Magic,

and the Spirit of

Adventure,

Always

Chapter One

"Now just a minute!" Lise Dawson exclaimed, grabbing for the handle of her carry-on bag. Dry, warm fingers met her grip instead, the touch of the man's skin adding fire to her heat.

His eyes weren't on fire. They were as dark and cold as the black ice on the roads back home. It was incredible they didn't melt in a climate like Papua New Guinea's.

"Listen, lady—"

His voice sent icy shivers skittering along her shoulder blades and down her arms. Slowly, she withdrew her fingers.

"—we don't have time for this."

She took a step backward, bumping up hard against a woman squatting on the airport floor nursing her baby. Mouthing an apology, Lise drew herself up to her full height, then turned back to Simon McDowell. She was tall, but not tall enough to reach past his chin.

"I'm not going anywhere without the rest of my luggage," she said adamantly.

"If you're coming with me," he said, tugging

his wide-brimmed hat lower over his eyes and turning away, "you're going to have to. I'm not waiting."

As he turned, an angry scar became visible. It streaked down and across his left cheek, toward the black hair curling incongruously around the edges of his angular face.

What had he done to get a scar like that?

Perspiration trickled down Lise's neck and rolled between her breasts, seeping damply into her cotton dress. She plucked the wet fabric away from her body. She'd come halfway around the world to avoid thinking about things medical. Coming to New Guinea had better not be a mistake. It felt like one.

"Mr. McDowell—"

"Simon," he barked, turning back. "Your Aunt Cecile and I are friends. She's the only damn reason I'm still standing here talking when we should be in the air."

"Simon," Lise amended, clinging fiercely to her temper. "What's the rush? Surely we can wait!"

"Mount Hagen has no night runway lights."

Lise stared at him, his words making no sense.

"When the sun goes down this close to the equator it sinks like a stone in water."

Eyes as dark as his should not be filled with so

much light.

"Unless we get to Mount Hagen before night falls," he added impatiently, "we can't land."

"Then I'll spend the night in Port Moresby and you can get going," Lise snapped, sweeping her heavy hair back from her damp forehead. One black curl escaped, cascading in front of her eyes. Her hair was unruly, had always behaved as though it possessed a life and will of its own. She snatched the curl between two fingers and dragged it back with the rest. Time to cut it, maybe. Change that, too. She had already changed everything else.

"Look, Miss Dawson—"

"Lise," she corrected.

"Lise," he growled. "Forget about your luggage. It'll follow you to the highlands tomorrow. I promised your aunt I'd deliver you safely and that's what I intend to do!"

Fatigue washed over Lise. She didn't have the energy to fight the man. All she really wanted was a warm hug from Aunt Cecile, a long soak in a tub full of cool water, and at least twenty hours sleep in a soft bed. A night in a strange hotel in Port Moresby was not on her list.

"All right," she capitulated. "Since you've come all this way to get me, I'll go with you."

"I didn't come to get you," Simon said. "You

were on my way." He turned and strode toward the airport door so quickly Lise had to run to catch up. "Your aunt phoned me last night in Sydney."

"About me?"

"No." His shoulders stiffened. "My nephew is sick."

"Where are his parents?"

"Dead."

Death. So final. "Your nephew lives with you?" she whispered.

"Connor's been my ward since he was a baby."

"What's the matter with him?" Lise asked. Her head began to spin. Faster and faster it twirled, the fans whirling overhead seeming slow by comparison. Her throat tightened with shame at her own cowardice.

"Malaria."

"Is he in the hospital?" Visions of long white hallways and excruciating decisions haunted her. Always wondering whether she'd made the right diagnosis, never sure until she was already committed to a course of action. Lise swallowed hard. Never knowing whether her patient would live or die.

"Hospital!" Simon laughed bitterly. "We don't have a hospital in the Waghi Valley." He flung open a door, revealing runways beyond. "And when we do, there'll be no doctors to run it."

Lise caught her breath. Simon's eyebrows were drawn together in a straight line above his eyes; storm clouds above a volcano. She edged through the doorway past him, afraid even one small movement would cause him to explode.

"But standing here won't make it happen," he said, taking hold of her elbow and pushing her ahead of him, "any more than my trip down south did." Something like electricity shafted from his fingers to her arm, then on through to her chest, stunning her.

Then came a blast of heat, slamming into her like a wall the moment she was through the door, drying up the question forming on her lips, and sucking out her body's moisture through every pore. Heat so different from the humidity created inside by countless perspiring passengers.

The tarmac stuck to the soles of her sandals, pulling at her, slowing her. After one swift glance in her direction, Simon reduced his pace, leading her off to the side of the terminal building away from the main runway area. Within minutes, he halted in front of a fragile-looking two-seater.

Lise's stomach lurched.

"What's the matter?" Simon demanded.

"It's awfully small," Lise said, despising the fear in her voice, willing it to disappear.

"Were you expecting a commercial jet?" he asked with a smile.

Maybe not a jet, but something bigger, more solid. Safer. Even when she'd flown in to her father's remote Montana ranch the planes had been larger than this.

Simon jerked open the door. "Time to go," he said, flinging his jacket and their carry-on bags behind the passenger seat. Then, without warning, he took Lise by the elbow and propelled her up the metal steps into the plane.

She watched through the window as Simon ducked under the nose and climbed in the other side. She'd been right. The plane was too small. There was scarcely an inch between them. Simon's leg muscles corded tensely, pushing against the corduroy of his pants. If she put out her hand, she could touch those muscles, smooth them.

She jerked her gaze away, leaned as far from Simon as possible, and stared out her window. Suddenly, his arm was around her, strong and compelling. With a sharp cry of protest, she pushed it away.

"Seat belt," he explained, his eyes amused now, also. "Get it on."

Heat climbed her throat and spread like fire across her cheeks. Would he guess she'd been thinking of touching him?

"Don't worry," he continued, his lips close to her ear. "I wasn't trying to seduce you."

Lise's hand stole up her neck, to the opal hanging there from a gold chain. The stone had been her mother's. The touch of its polished surface usually gave her strength. Not this time.

With what seemed deliberate slowness, Simon turned to the controls and flicked some switches. The engine roared to life and they taxied onto the runway. They gradually gathered speed, the plane churning along the paved surface until it rose into the air like a bird.

Lise forced her hands to remain in her lap; didn't allow them to clutch at anything, determined not to let him know her fear. There was nothing to hold onto anyway, just a stubby leather strap hanging from the ceiling. Was it there for emergencies, or everyday use?

The engine's roar softened as Simon pulled the plane out of its climb and circled the hot, dry hills of Port Moresby before heading out over the greenest trees Lise had ever seen, away from the ocean and up toward the highlands.

She closed her eyes and tried not to think about the jagged rocks poking through the blanket of trees below. Home seemed a long way away.

Her throat thickened.

She didn't have a home.

"Are you asleep?"

She snapped her eyes open.

"For a tourist, you're not showing much interest in the countryside."

"I'm not here as a tourist," she said, frowning.

"What then?"

"I'm here to see my aunt." Hopefully, Cecile could fix the pain in her heart.

"But you can't fly over the most primitive country in the world and not look!"

Lise forced herself to quickly glance out the window, fighting back a rush of panic.

"Right," she said, turning swiftly away from the glass. "I looked."

He laughed.

A heat burst through Lise, as sudden and inexplicable as her desire to hear him laugh like that again. The window beside her was tiny, but that didn't stop the afternoon sun from pouring in. Like sitting in a furnace. That's what was making her hot. It wasn't Simon McDowell at all. Lise raised her arms above her head and forced her curls into a cooler knot.

She glanced out the window again, resolutely keeping her gaze away from McDowell. With any luck, they would soon be safely there.

Safe. There seemed nothing safe about this man her aunt had sent. With that scar, he appeared . . . dangerous.

She pursed her lips. There was probably some simple explanation as to how he had gotten it, nothing dangerous at all.

"How did you hurt your face?" she asked, wincing after she'd done so, the question escaping her lips before she could stop it.

She knew better than to ask personal questions. Especially of men. They didn't like talking about their injuries, particularly visible ones.

McDowell shrugged, his hands never leaving the controls. "I had a run-in with a bad driver," he explained.

"A car accident?"

"I was in a race." He glanced at her, his gaze leaving the control panel for only an instant. "The Banz Motorcross."

"You were racing a motorcycle?"

"Why not? It's exciting."

Lise bit the inside of her cheek. A man willing to risk his life for a bit of excitement. A man like her father. She swallowed hard. Simon McDowell was obviously not someone she could afford to know better. She didn't need, or want, the kind of pain a man like him could bring.

She glanced at her lap. Her fingers were clenched into a tight ball. She slowly flexed them, at the same time drawing in a deep breath. She held the air a few seconds, then released it, praying the tension in her body would dissipate.

She could feel it working, until Simon leaned toward her again, his lips just inches from her own. Involuntarily, she raised her hand, desperate to put something, anything, between them.

"Bad weather coming," was all he said, reaching across her and pointing out her window. A dark cloud was forming against the mountains to the east, spreading in their direction.

"Is it dangerous?"

He shook his head.

His denial did nothing to quell her stomach's churning. She had only just met Simon, but if she were right about the sort of man he was, a storm would be just the kind of challenge he would enjoy.

But why was he frowning? "What's the matter?" she demanded.

He swept his hand through his hair, blocking his face.

"You're worrying about Connor," she guessed, sympathy pushing aside fear.

"He'll be fine," Simon said tightly.

"Has he had malaria before?" Her questions were automatic. She'd been good at this once.

"Twice." Simon's face darkened. "He's one of the reasons we need a hospital."

She didn't want to talk about hospitals.

"People in developed nations—" Simon shot her a swift glance. "—haven't got a clue. They take it all for granted. Education, health services. Everything's there for the asking. But in a country like New Guinea a bout with malaria can kill you."

"If the valley needs a hospital, surely the government will provide it."

He shook his head. "The government has enough on its plate. They say they'll help all they can, but when? Ten years from now? Twenty? That's not good enough."

It wasn't, either. Little boys like Connor . . . Lise blocked the picture from her mind. Couldn't bear to examine it.

Simon's face grew bleak. "When there's an emergency, you need help fast."

Fast. The air sped from Lise's lungs. She shut her eyes, but this time couldn't stop the image from flooding in . . . her father lying on the ground bleeding . . .

Fast didn't necessarily save anyone. Perspiration broke out on her brow. She tugged a hankie from her dress pocket and wiped her forehead. She had to pull herself together, had to stop all this thinking.

"What can you do about it?" she asked, forcing her attention away from her memories. Simon didn't seem the type to wait for others to take action.

"I went to Sydney looking for funding and medical staff."

"Did you succeed?"

"Marginally." His lips tightened to a thin line, and a muscle along his jawline jumped. "Bloody doctors!" He pounded his fist against his thigh. "None of those I interviewed were prepared to practice in an under-developed country for any length of time." He shook his head in disgust. "Too interested in life in the big city." His gaze seemed to turn inward. "Stupid to have expected anything different."

"I can't believe there weren't—"

"What would you know about it?" he demanded, his gaze back on her.

More than she cared to know.

"The reality is most people don't care." He kneaded his fingers against his brow, as though the effort to explain were too much, as though he were filled with a pain too deep for words. "They don't want to be isolated. They don't want to make any long-term commitments." He paused. "They don't even want to try."

"I don't believe that," Lise protested. "There must be plenty of doctors who would want to work here." Other doctors. Those who hadn't lost their nerve.

"And you've been in New Guinea how long?" Simon asked, his lips twisting. "Half a day?"

Lise slumped against her seat. This trip was supposed to be a retreat, not a nightmare. She needed refuge, not abuse. She had dumped more than enough of that on herself already. She glanced at Simon, praying he would leave it now, praying he would drop all talk of things she couldn't discuss.

His chest rose, then fell again, as though the physical act of filling and emptying his lungs soothed him, exorcised the demons she had seen so clearly in his eyes. He stared at the ground below.

"There it is," he said, his voice softening. "The Waghi Valley. Some say it's the most beautiful valley in the world." He turned, and her heart beat faster at the sight of his smile. "And I'm one of them. But judge for yourself." He did something to the controls and the world outside went crazy.

A flash of sunlight reflected off the wings as the sky turned upside down. Lise reached out wildly, desperate for something to hold on to. Her hand met Simon's pants, his leg strong and warm and reassuring beneath the thick corduroy.

The plane slipped through the air, left wing tip pointed straight at the ground. Her body strained against the seat belt. Any second now, she'd be right in his lap. She couldn't seem to get enough air. Her heart seemed intent on hammering its way through her chest.

For a single moment that seemed to last a lifetime, her gaze was riveted through the window. The earth seemed as though it were rising to meet her. She pressed her eyes shut.

"Why aren't you looking?"

Forcing her eyes open, she stared incredulously at him. "You turned us upside down on purpose?"

"We're hardly upside down. This is the only way to see the ground properly in a low wing plane."

"Put it back the way it was." Lise gritted her teeth. "Please."

The plane righted with a sickening lurch. She lifted her hand to her face. Her lips were trembling and the blood must have drained from her cheeks, for there was no heat there at all. She glared at Simon. "Don't do that again!"

His lips twitched. "Does that mean you'll be coming up with me again? Next Sunday, perhaps?"

"Never!"

He chuckled.

Angrily, she turned away and peered out the window. She could see just fine, thank you very much, without being turned upside down. He was right about one thing, though. It was a beautiful sight. Bushes shimmered in the waning sunlight. Smoke rose from the huts of scattered villages. Fields, growing something vine-like . . .

"Kaukau," Simon said, as though reading her thoughts. "Sweet potato. The life blood of the people here. It takes months to grow, and if the crops fail they starve."

The kaukau fields were everywhere. And snaking through the middle of them was a river, reeds and bulrushes hiding its banks as it twisted and turned.

"Don't let the river's beauty fool you," he cautioned. "The Waghi's full of deadly currents. It claims its share."

If he was trying to scare her, he was doing a good job.

"Tourists come here expecting the same rules to apply as they do back home. But the tropics are different. The sun is hotter, the rains heavier—" He caught her gaze again. "And the people more fierce. Unless you're careful, you can end up with real problems."

She already had real problems.

"Were you serious when you said you were staying?" His tone implied he didn't believe her, that he expected she'd be gone on the next plane.

"I'll be here a while," Lise muttered, averting her gaze from his face. For however long it took to heal, assuming that was even possible.

The sun was lower on the horizon now. It shone through the front window and straight into Lise's eyes, blinding her. But when she looked down, she could see too much. The airstrip on which they were supposed to land seemed too narrow, too short. She clung to the edge of her seat as the ground rose to meet them, but the plane touched down with no more than a bump, then gently rolled toward the airport building.

On the ground at last. Lise let out the breath she hadn't been aware of holding and turned to Simon. "Thanks for the lift."

"You're welcome."

Now the ride was over, she could relax, would make herself relax. "It'll be good to see

Aunt Cecile," she said, feeling better at the mere thought. "I haven't seen her in years, but from her letters and all the pictures she's sent, she hasn't changed much. Except for the nun's habit, of course." She was babbling, but couldn't seem to stop.

"She's doing a good job running the Vocational school."

"How do you know her?" Lise asked.

"We're neighbors, of sorts."

The plane jolted over a bump and came to a stop. Lise peered through the window toward the terminal. "I don't see her. She must be waiting inside."

Simon pushed back his hat and faced her. "Didn't I mention?" His eyebrows lifted innocently. "I'm driving you to the mission."

Chapter Two

"How high up is the Waghi Valley?"

Why had the woman even bothered to ask? She couldn't possibly care. She was sitting the way Marion had always sat, one silk-clad leg crossed over the other. Except this woman's legs were even better than his ex-wife's. This woman's legs could drive a man mad. Simon's lips tightened. There was no way any woman was going to drive him mad again.

"Five thousand feet," he muttered, casting a swift glance at Lise. He'd been right about her not caring. Her face had a glazed look about it, reminding him of Marion's when he'd talked about New Guinea.

A familiar pain twisted his heart. He leaned closer to his door to let the sun warm his face. The heat was still intense, though shortly it would be gone altogether. He loved this time of day. There was a stillness about it; a peace. Although God knows he didn't feel much of that at the moment. Not with Conner sick. But he couldn't think about the boy now.

He was going as fast as he could. Probably too

fast, judging from the expression on Lise's face every time they hit a bump on the dirt road.

"Will we be there before dark?" she asked.

"I hope so," Simon muttered. It was tough enough sitting next to a woman like her in broad daylight. Sitting next to her in the dark would be impossible. He risked another glance.

Her lips were pursed, no doubt assessing the probability of a score of servants waiting at the other end to draw her bath and see to her every comfort.

A second spasm of pain caught him unawares. The one thing Marion had enjoyed about New Guinea was plantation life. She had loved the parties at the club, hosting dinners for friends and going to their houses in return. She had made him love it, too.

But it hadn't been enough to make Marion stay. He hadn't been enough. Not once her work was finished. The pain shafted deeper, catching him under the ribs, making it difficult to breathe. Even Connor hadn't made the difference. Marion pretended to enjoy the baby at first. For a long time, Simon deluded himself that Connor would become as important to Marion as he was to him.

He had been wrong. Hardly Marion's fault. Not everyone was cut out to be a mother, but he should have guessed from the way Marion behaved with Connor that she'd do what she did.

"How often do you make the trip into Mount Hagen?" Lise asked.

He had to look at her a moment before he could answer, focus on her eyes to push back the smothering blanket of memories.

"Not often," he finally managed. Never often enough to suit Marion. And from the looks of this woman with her red-tipped nails and stylish clothes, it wouldn't be enough for her, either. Thank God, she wasn't his concern.

Simon wrenched the wheel to one side, but wasn't quick enough to stop the Jeep plowing through an enormous pot hole. It lurched, then bumped, then shook and rattled before he brought it under control again.

Lise bumped against him and his breath caught as her hand grazed his shoulder. He couldn't feel her skin through his shirt, but he could feel her warmth. Her touch lasted only an instant, but the heat lingered like the taste of fine wine.

"Damn," he swore, the car still shuddering. He swerved onto the shoulder of the road, avoiding a young girl herding two pigs in front of her with the help of a big stick.

Clamping down on the brakes, he stopped the car, then looked at Lise again to make sure she was all right.

"Do you have to drive like a maniac?" she demanded, her face as white as the lace on the collar of her dress. She raised her hand and gingerly touched her lip. A spot of blood rubbed off onto her finger.

Simon shoved his hand into his pants' pocket and pulled out his handkerchief, offering it to her. She seemed too stunned to take it, like a rabbit caught in the beam of a headlight. He could almost see her heart hammering against her chest.

Slowly, so as not to frighten her further, he brought his handkerchief toward her lip. She glared at him, probably furious the roads weren't paved, but neither her look nor his own inclination could stop his fingers from approaching those lips. He had to touch them, to see if they were as soft, as warm, as they looked.

They were.

She sat motionless. She didn't blink. She didn't flinch. She seemed to set her jaw and, with enormous effort of will, remain still. There had been a few women since Marion left, but not one of them had made him feel like this. Protective. Concerned.

His head felt light. It wasn't so much that he'd let out his breath as that he'd stopped breathing altogether and didn't know how to begin again. He wrenched his hand from her lips.

"Thank you," Lise said, her voice strained, staring straight ahead.

"Better now?" Simon asked, clamping both his hands on the wheel.

"I'm fine."

"Good." He switched on the ignition. "Hang on this time." Perhaps speed would wipe the memory of her softness from his brain.

"You're going to hit someone!" she cried, her voice reaching him over the sound of fast tires on gravel.

"Better pray I don't." The speed wasn't helping. He glanced at her. She still looked sick. He slowed the Jeep. "If I do hit someone," he explained, "or even a pig, you'd better head to the nearest airport and catch the next flight out of the country. The people here demand an eye for an eye."

"Are you joking?"

She sounded frightened, but she hadn't been born here. She would never get beyond the strangeness and fear to know the wonder of the place. Marion hadn't, for all the probing she had done into the lives of the people. But with

Marion, the knowledge had been in her head only, never in her heart.

"Better learn the local customs," he growled, turning away as he spoke. Lise would be going back to her own country soon, long before she learned any customs. Loneliness seeped over Simon, chilling him.

Lise clamped her lips shut and stared through the glass in front of her. She didn't want to learn anything from Simon. The sooner this ride was over, the better. Dust drifted through the floorboards of the Jeep and in through the open windows, settling on her like a fine mist. The people trudging along the side of the road were covered in it, the dust turning their brown skin grey.

"Highlanders are different from the coastal people," Simon explained.

What he said seemed true. These men were shorter, stockier, stronger, and fiercer. Their curly, black beards were eye-catching, virile. Virile. Like Simon was virile.

She shivered, remembering the touch of his hand, struggling to forget it.

The highlanders strode along the side of the road in single file. Long, wide grass, bunched and tied at the waist, spread out over their buttocks like a fan. Bamboo necklaces hung from their necks, and thin shells protruded from the holes pierced in their noses and ears.

Their faces were arrogant. Like Simon's. She glanced at him. No, not nearly so much as Simon's.

He shifted toward her on the seat and rummaged in his back pocket for something as he drove. His shoulder almost touched her.

"Simon—" Desperately, she searched for something to say, something to take her mind off his nearness. She gestured to some women walking along a footpath. Heavily laden bags hung from their foreheads, falling over their backs.

"What are they carrying in those bags?"

He needed only a glance. "Those are bilum bags."

The women wore nothing from the waist up. Their naked breasts hung loose, swaying with the rhythm of their movements.

"They roll the inner layer of tree bark into string, then weave the string into bags."

Lise watched his lips as he spoke.

Simon shifted down a gear and slowed the Jeep. "They carry kaukau in them, pounds of it, firewood, whatever they need."

Pouting lips. Sexy.

He turned to her then, his face stern. "It's a

tough life for women in this country."

He'd already warned her of that. Lise shifted her gaze to the woman in front. Her bilum didn't appear to be full of wood. It was softer and spread wide at the bottom.

"What's she carrying," Lise asked, wanting to know, not wanting to slip into anything personal with this man.

He sharply drew in a breath and, once again, pain flickered across his face. "She has a baby in there," he muttered, then stared at the road ahead, his face a mask.

Lise frowned. The pain had disappeared so quickly, she couldn't be sure she had even seen it, but there was one thing she now knew and it startled her. Simon cared for these people yet seemed too controlled a man to care this much.

"Tired?" he asked.

"Yes," she replied, fatigue gripping her. "But I'm glad I'm here."

He turned to her, his eyes filled with disbelief. It irritated her, made her want to explain.

"You know—" She faltered, then lifting her chin, she tried again. "I'm looking forward to seeing my aunt, to live a new life for a while."

His eyebrows drew together. "Was the old one so bad?"

She didn't want to talk about that. Not now.

Not with him. She turned her face away. He must be able to hear the pounding of her heart. She'd heard of easy silences between a man and a woman, but there was nothing easy about this.

He stepped hard on the gas pedal. A large rock, flung up by the tires, thumped against the floorboards immediately below her feet. It saved her from having to answer. Nobody could be expected to talk while hurtling along this gravel road.

It was going to rain. Black clouds were building overhead, the sky growing more somber by the minute. Like Simon.

She shivered, not just her arms this time, but her whole body. Drops, like wet bullets, hit the window pane. Hastily, she wound up her window. In the seconds it took for Simon to turn on the wipers, tiny rivers had streamed through the dust blanketing the windows.

"Can you see?" she asked.

"Well enough," he answered, peering ahead. He waved a hand toward the sky. "The monsoons. The rain starts every day about this time. I'd hoped to get past the river before it began." He stomped hard on the brake. "Damn!"

A line of trucks had somehow accumulated in front of them and were now backing toward them. Simon swore again, reversed, and edged carefully backward. Then, as suddenly as he had started, he stopped.

Lise flattened herself against the seat, sure the trucks in front would ram them, but one by one they turned off onto a narrow road on Simon's right. The road before them cleared. She relaxed, barely able to see fifty yards ahead in the downpour, but reassured now that no one was going to hit them.

Simon pressed on the gas, and the Jeep shot forward in the direction the trucks had rejected, fish-tailing on the now muddy road.

"Where are you going?" Lise demanded.

Ahead of them was the river, wider than it had looked from the sky and twice as turbulent. A wooden slatted bridge spanned the distance across—or at least, used to span the distance. Like broken twigs, two of the planks hung in the middle, their jagged edges showing yellow and raw against the darkened sky.

"Damn," Simon swore. He brought the Jeep to a shuddering halt.

"Is there another way across?" Lise asked, trying not to imagine being on the bridge when it collapsed.

"Yes."

"Thank heavens!"

"Forty-five minutes south of here, then forty-five minutes back on the other side." Simon's voice was grimmer than his face.

Lise's heart sank. An hour-and-a-half extra. If they were lucky.

A drop of water splattered against her hair. The rain was driving through at the edges of the window, then beading and dripping down the pane. Her cotton dress seemed suddenly flimsy.

Simon turned to face her. "We'll have to go through it."

"Go through what?"

He backed up the Jeep, then shifted into its lowest gear. Wrenching the steering wheel to the right, he drove off the shoulder and down the slope toward the river.

"What are you doing?" Lise shrieked, clutching the door handle to keep from sliding off her seat.

"Crossing the river." His lips curved into a grin.

"The Waghi?" she asked, terror surging through her.

"One of its tributaries." He shrugged. "I have to get home."

The Jeep lurched over a hump on the hill and tilted precariously.

He was crazy! No, he was loving this. It showed on his face. Well, she wasn't having any part of it. She hadn't flown thousands of miles to drown in a river.

"Let me out!" she demanded.

The water's edge loomed frighteningly close.

He didn't even slow.

She grabbed the door handle and twisted. She had managed to open it a crack when strong fingers clamped down on her wrist.

"Don't be a fool."

The weight of Simon's arm pinned her body against her seat. He glared at her, his eyes blacker than the sky. She fought the strength of his gaze. Fought him.

He stepped hard on the brake, the Jeep half-sliding, half-grinding to a halt. They were poised, angled downward, the water mere inches away.

"Shut the door, Lise."

She hesitated, already frozen from the downpour forcing its way in. Then she slammed the door shut, keeping her fingers on the handle.

"I won't go through that river," she said fiercely, gritting her jaw to stop it from trembling.

"What do you plan to do?" he demanded. "Walk? We're miles from town. It's raining!"

The front window was awash with water. It was falling faster than the wipers could sweep it away.

He glanced at her feet. "Those sandals you're wearing won't last you five minutes." His gaze traveled to her face. "Well?"

She parted her lips to tell him anything was better than driving deliberately into that foaming expanse, but a tentacle of fear froze her tongue. She couldn't go into that river, but to leap out alone into an unknown countryside, filled with unknown people, in the sort of weather she had seen only in movies, was more than she could face.

"Smart choice." Simon released her arm, lifted his foot from the brake and steered the Jeep into the river.

Lise let go of the door, grabbing the dashboard with one hand and the edge of her leather seat with the other.

Any minute now water would come pouring through the floorboards. Her legs stiff, she braced herself against a floor she didn't want to touch.

She was breathing too fast, too shallowly. Her head felt light, almost dizzy. Take deep breaths. Deep, slow breaths. Calm down . . . calmer. If the Jeep overturned, she had to be ready.

She risked a glance at Simon. His hands held the steering wheel loosely. His feet were steady and sure on the pedals.

Rocks crunched noisily beneath the tires. What if she stopped hearing them? Would the Jeep sink into river mud and disappear for ever?

She was a decent swimmer, but to swim in a flooding river was beyond her abilities. The current would grip her and drag her away.

She twisted and peered out the rear window. The back tires were in the water now. A thick tree branch thumped against the Jeep, then swirled behind it, snagging onto the shore they'd just left. Lise tried to swallow, but couldn't.

The Jeep lurched toward the downstream side, slipping like a child on ice. She clutched her handholds more tightly.

"Okay, Simon. Please turn back now."

"No going back." His gaze was fixed firmly on the river in front of him. "Just relax."

Her fingers were numb from the pressure of holding on.

"This is a shallow stretch."

"What do you call deep?" she demanded.

"How do you think they got across these rivers before the bridges were built?"

With ropes and long lines of sure-footed New Guinea tribesmen. She had seen the documentaries.

"The trick is to keep moving slowly."

"There's a trick to this?"

"If we stop, we stall. Then we'll be in trouble." He turned to her, his gaze scanning her face. Unbelievably, his expression softened, lightening from coal black to the darkness of a cave, safe and secure.

"I'll take care of you."

She almost believed him.

"Everything will be fine."

She had heard that before. From her father. If she could simply shut her eyes and keep them shut until they were on the other side. But she couldn't stop staring at the water. It was a frothing, living power, carrying branches, plants, rocks and flotsam toward them. A cold wetness licked her feet through her open-toed sandals.

"Simon," she croaked, panic snaking through her. She unclenched her fingers long enough to point toward the water around her feet. His feet were dry, propped against the pedals and encased in thick shoes.

"We'll be all right, Lise. It's not that deep."

"But it's fast." Her mind shied away from the reality of her words.

"We'll be there in no time. We're half-way there already."

It was true. As they drove, the river seemed to part around Simon's Jeep. She glanced again at the water lapping her toes. No, not parted exactly. But, halfway! The leaden feeling in her chest lifted slightly. Perhaps they could make it.

Thump.

The sound jarred Lise's bones. She bit back a scream.

They must have banged against a boulder. A big one.

The Jeep shifted heavily to one side.

She flung out her arm to steady herself, fighting an overwhelming need to grab hold of Simon. Her hand brushed his arm, then recoiled.

The noise. Her head pounded from the roar. Opening her eyes wide, she struggled to determine where the rain left off and the river began.

Then she closed her eyes, anxious to shut out the terrifying turbulence. Another jolt and she reached forward blindly, needing something, anything, to halt her headlong rush into panic.

Hard metal. At last. Something solid. Secure. Immovable.

It moved.

Another thud. Another boulder. Then no movement at all, not forward, not backward, not even sideways.

"Now you've done it," Simon said, his voice icy.

Reluctantly, Lise opened her eyes.

The steering wheel. Her hand was locked on

the steering wheel. And Simon's face was even colder than his voice.

She sucked in a deep breath.

"I told you to hang on, not try to steer."

She unglued her fingers from the wheel.

"Well, you got your wish, Lise. We walk!"

Simon jerked open his door and stepped out into the maelstrom as though it were nothing. The rain separated him from her, falling in sheets around him, plastering his black hair to his skull like a cap. Then he turned to face her, holding out his hand.

"Come on," he shouted. "Out my side."

She could hear neither him nor the flooding river. The pounding of her own heart eliminated all sound.

She stared past him. Froth, thrown up by the current, looked like fingers ready to pull her under. Lise shuddered. She couldn't do it. Nothing could make her.

She stared back at Simon. His eyes were hard, unrelenting, insistent.

They could make her.

She ignored his hand and slid along the seat toward his door. She swung her legs out, then stopped, unable to force herself further. She was breathing too quickly. She'd hyper-ventilate if she wasn't careful. Sucking in one slow, ragged breath, she tried again.

The water looked freezing cold. Drowning, hypothermia, she'd seen them all at the hospital. But this was the tropics. How cold could it be? With great effort, she forced one foot down, then yanked it up again.

That cold.

She might have imagined the blur of his body as he moved toward her, but the warmth of Simon's arms as he plucked her off the seat was real.

For an instant, she allowed herself to cling to him, relief sweeping over her as insistently as fear. His strength was rock solid, his body a haven.

Haven? Lise loosened her grip from around Simon's neck. He was no haven. Her heart sped faster. He was more dangerous than the river.

"Hang on," he growled. "Or can't you bloody well even do that?"

"Put me down," she demanded.

"Can't." He grinned. "Your aunt would never forgive me. We'll just have to make the best of this." He held her around her back and under her legs.

Unable to stop herself, Lise tightened her grip around Simon's neck. She held her breath as he took his first step forward.

How could he see? Her body must be blocking his view of the river bottom, and the water was over his knees. The rain stung her eyes but she forced them open wide enough to peer down at the water. The swirling silt and debris on the surface revealed nothing of what was below.

If he stumbled, they'd both tumble in, although they couldn't get any wetter than they already were. Her dress clung to her skin, its thin cotton now virtually transparent.

"Cold?" Simon murmured, his breath fanning her cheek. "We'll be out of here soon."

The heat from his lips threatened to draw hers to them. His chin, rough with afternoon stubble, brushed against her forehead as she turned her face to his chest.

She tried to clear her mind of everything—the river, the storm, the man—but she couldn't escape. When she breathed, she breathed him in, the faint scent of his after-shave combining with the fresh smell of rain.

Her heart thumped against his chest. Or was it his heart against hers?

He stumbled, caught himself, then clasped her more closely. Her skin smoldered where her body touched his.

She risked another glance at the paralyzingly

swift current. The water swirled past Simon's thighs, now seeming to pull at him. They had been tugged a few feet downstream, off the more shallow course in which Simon had directed the car.

The sky was blacker now than when they'd entered the water. Soon it would be dark.

Then suddenly, incredibly, they were all but there. Just a few more yards.

"You can put me down now," Lise whispered, Simon's neck tight with strain beneath her clasped hands.

"Not until we get to shore."

"Why on earth didn't you take the other road?"

A drop of water fell from his tangled hair onto her cheek and a mischievous glint appeared in his eyes. "Much more fun this way," he said, grinning at her.

"Fun! How can you even pretend this is fun?" Lise untangled her frigid fingers and slipped her arms from around his neck. Pushing against his chest, she attempted to wiggle her legs free from his arms.

He surged forward and dumped her on the bank of the river. Then without uttering a word, he fought his way back through the water toward the Jeep.

A violent shiver surged across her shoulders, the cold gnawing deep into her bones. How could he go back? It was all she could do to stand.

Vaguely, she became aware of a truck parked on the roadway. The two men in it were staring at her as though she were some sort of river spirit. She must look dreadful, dress clinging, sandals limp and broken. One more thing Simon had been right about.

He moved much faster without her. In no time at all he was at the Jeep, pulling a rope from the back and tying it to the front. He grabbed something from inside, then struggled toward her, playing out the rope as he walked.

The two men climbed down from their truck and moved toward the water's edge. Simon flung them the end of the rope and they tied it to their vehicle.

Lise sank down onto the rocks, her arms wrapped around her body. Simon strode up the bank toward her, his eyes burning like two fires in a pit.

"Here," he said, pulling her to her feet. "Put this on."

He draped his wool-lined jacket over her shoulders. It fell, too large, too long, but very warm around her body.

Chapter Three

Lise tugged fiercely at the stubborn weed, but still it clung to the soil. Gritting her teeth, she tried again, pulling so hard that when it finally gave way, she had to fling out one hand to keep herself from falling.

She scowled at the tenacious bit of greenery. Who was it had said gardening was relaxing? They had lied. Or maybe it was all in the technique. She sighed. Whatever the truth of it, she needed this now. Needed the hard work and sweat. Needed something to stop her from thinking.

She ran the back of her hand across her forehead and squinted at the sky. The sun was pale yellow, not brilliant at all, but its rays were hot for this early in the day.

She pressed her eyes shut. Simon's jacket had been warm, too, though not nearly so warm as the touch of his skin. She could still remember that warmth. Had thought of little else for the past three days.

Perhaps if she worked harder.

It was ridiculous. She had come to New

Guinea to relax. To decide what to do with the rest of her life.

Sounded dramatic put like that but she didn't have many options. Should she take the research position she'd been offered? She would have to decide soon. Within a month at the most, as the position came open in three months time. The interview had gone well, though she'd been so frozen inside she could scarcely remember the responses she had made to their questions. There was only one thing of which she was sure. She could not go into practice.

Aunt Cecile's setters raced out of the shrubbery at the back of the garden and barked frantically as they tore around to the front of the house. Lise flung a last handful of weeds onto the clippings pile, and stood, her back stiffening as she straightened. It felt good to get back to more physical work, though she wasn't accustomed to it anymore. Not since she had left home for university. On the ranch there had always been plenty to do, although her father hadn't bothered much with flowers since her mother had died.

Lise followed the dogs around the house, not surprised when they streaked down the drive toward the gate. A battered blue pick-up truck was parked at the entrance.

Whoever it was wasn't getting out. Must be a man. The dogs only barked at men. A sudden shiver trickled the length of her spine.

The man better not be Simon.

Aunt Cecile's piercing whistle halted the dog's din.

They ran back to the house as quickly as they had left it, splitting around Lise as they passed her. She continued to the end of the drive and swung the gate wide. A pair of grey eyes set in a brown weathered face stared curiously down at her from the truck's cab, then the man smiled his thanks and drove past her to the house. Closing the gate, Lise followed.

"Cecile, you've got to do something about those dogs," the man complained, swinging his legs out of the cab. He ran one hand through his long, sandy hair.

Lise giggled. From the way he spoke, this was not the first time the visitor had made the complaint.

"I will not!" her aunt refused, brown eyes flashing as she made her way down the steps from the porch. "We're an all female establishment. These dogs are our protection against intruders." She smiled at the three panting beasts at her feet. "I can't help it if they don't like men."

The man shook his head in mock despair, then turned to Lise, his eyes twinkling. "Hello," he said, thrusting out his right hand. "I'm Brother Michael."

~*~

Lise settled onto the cracked leather seat of Michael's truck, a truck he drove at a snail's pace. She'd taken him up on his invitation to accompany his high school class on their field trip.

She twisted her neck and peeked through the narrow glass window at the boys squeezed into the back of the open truck. Bright flowers and an assortment of pencils and pens poked out at odd angles from their tightly curled hair.

There were no girls in the class. They had their own school on the other side of Mount Hagen, Brother Michael had explained.

The boys were a handsome lot, all stocky and strong and gleaming with health, although a few had festering leg infections. Those sores needed to be looked at, and soon.

But not by her. Not now. The school must have someone to take care of such things. Lise's fingers clenched as a familiar wave of guilt swept over her.

Michael slowed the truck even further as they neared the end of the mission's long driveway.

"That's one of our property boundaries," he said, pointing to a small river running parallel to the drive. "We'll be touring the coffee plantation on the other side. It's owner, Simon McDowell, is on the high school's Board of Directors."

Simon McDowell.

Michael swung the truck onto the main road and continued to chat about his students. Lise only half-listened, her mind shying from the prospect of seeing Simon again, yet filled with nothing else.

They trundled over a small bridge spanning the river, then swung to the left, down a twisting dirt driveway. Coffee bushes closed in on them from both sides. Red-skinned beans hung from the branches, glistening like holly berries at Christmas.

A nerve twitched at the corner of Lise's eye. Maybe Simon wouldn't be there. Surely, a plantation owner would be too busy to lead a pack of school boys around on a tour. He would delegate that to someone else.

Her throat was dry by the time they emerged from the bushes and drew up in front of the coffee factory's tall wooden walls. Simon appeared at the open office door, his smile of welcome fading when his gaze met hers.

She lifted her chin and prayed her face didn't

look as drawn and pinched as her insides felt.

Simon approached the truck. "Sightseeing, Miss Dawson?" He bent slightly to her open window.

"Seemed like the place to start," she replied tartly.

A ghost of a smile drifted across his lips. He opened her door but made no effort to move out of her way.

He was too close. She couldn't climb down from the cab without bumping into him. Even dressed in wide khaki shorts and hiking boots, he was as much in control as the day she met him.

She stared straight ahead, determined to avoid his eyes. Her breath caught as she found herself staring at his chest instead. The top three buttons of his shirt were undone, allowing myriad black hairs to curl through the opening. The pulse at the base of his throat throbbed.

The insolent curve of his lips drew her gaze to them, making her want to feel their heat. Her breath escaped in a rush.

She jerked her gaze higher. His eyes were unreadable, but the knowing expression on his face made it obvious he had seen what had been in hers. She blinked once, then shut her eyes.

She couldn't see him now, but she could smell

him. His scent was like the earth after a rain. Musky, yet clean.

She felt dizzy. What was Michael saying? She could scarcely make out his words, there was such a buzzing in her head.

". . . thought Lise might like to meet you . . . close neighbors and all."

"We've met."

She opened her eyes then, keeping her gaze resolutely on Simon's chest. His shirt was damp, as though he'd been working hard. Slowly, deliberately it seemed, he took a step backward. Lise swung out her legs and dropped to the ground. Behind her, the boys spilled from the truck like so many puppies, laughing and shaking the dust off their clothes. They surrounded Simon, separating him from her like a sandbar in the incoming tide.

His gaze met hers above the students' heads, but she could see no warmth at all in their dark depths. He turned toward the boys, a muscle jumping along his jaw. When he raised his hand, their chatter subsided.

Lise leaned back against the truck. He was ignoring her. Thank God. Then, without warning, he motioned her forward.

"Come with me, Miss Dawson," he said, his manner jocular, though his eyes challenged hers.

"Wouldn't want you to get lost."

"Hardly possible with such a guide." She forced a smile to her lips.

Several of the boys giggled, then glanced uncertainly in her direction. She stepped away from the truck. Uncomfortably aware of the many eyes upon her, she didn't allow her gaze to waver from Simon's face.

"Right this way," he said with a half-smile, sweeping his arm through the air and ending the gesture with an elaborate bow.

She stood motionless for a moment, uncertain, but he took her by the elbow and led her with him away from the factory. Her nerve-endings focused to where his fingers touched her skin, her arm alive with sensation. Could he feel it too?

He must. And from the expression on his face, it made him as uncomfortable as it did her. His stride quickened, forcing her to walk faster.

The boys fell in behind them, chattering and pushing. A well-rutted lane between two rows of coffee stretched ahead.

"The tractor can get through in the dry season," Simon said, beginning his explanation of the production process. "But now the monsoons are here they get bogged down. The ripe beans with red skins are called cherries."

Along with the others, Lise glanced toward the bushes. The cherries were close enough to pick, their shiny, hard surfaces resembling children's beads. Between the bushes, she caught a glimpse of the pickers, their hands flowing like water between branch and basket.

"The cherries are the ones we pick," Simon continued, his voice warming as he spoke. "We go through the bushes time after time while the coffee flush lasts, until we've got them all."

He seemed to miss nothing as they walked. She could see his mind working, assessing the crop, tallying the weight of the berries and the price they'd bring. His lips curved upward, his calculations apparently pleasing.

Suddenly, the green branches parted and a wizened brown woman emerged from between two bushes. She flashed a toothless grin. Simon jerked to a stop and released Lise's arm.

"Lucy, man bilong yu i stap we?" he demanded sharply.

"Em i go long ples lukim. Wanpela bigpela singsing i kamap," Lucy said, grinning as she spoke, yet sidling away from Simon's displeasure.

"What's going on?" Lise whispered to Michael.

"Her husband, who's supposed to be working,

has gone off to his village. It seems his people are having some sort of traditional ceremony."

Michael grimaced. "Simon doesn't look too pleased."

"Surely he doesn't begrudge his workers time off for important occasions?" she whispered, frowning.

"Not at all," Michael replied. "But it is the middle of coffee flush and apparently this fellow left without telling anyone. Simon has to be able to count on his pickers."

She watched as the old woman listened to Simon, nodded, then disappeared into the trees as soundlessly as she had emerged.

Lise pressed her lips together. Simon had treated the woman with respectful firmness, but Lise had been on the receiving end of his anger herself, and knew how it felt.

Simon turned and strode toward the factory, not seeming to care now if Lise kept up. She dropped back through the crowd of boys, trailing behind them, only catching up as the group peered into an enormous vat of swirling water. Its surface was bright with red coffee skins.

"We grind the cherries to loosen the skins, then wash them in these vats," Simon was explaining. "The red skins and faulty beans float to the surface and we sluice them away until only the good beans are left."

Lise stared down at the water. Things were deceptive here. Those pretty, red skins were utterly useless. Like she was now. The only decision she felt happy about lately had been the one to come to New Guinea.

And Simon McDowell was ruining that!

"We dry the beans in the open air for approximately three weeks," Simon continued, gesturing to row upon row of yellow plastic completely covered with coffee beans. "We close the plastic over them at night to keep off the dew." The thunder had disappeared from his face. He seemed even to be enjoying himself.

Her father had been the same. Nothing made him happier than to talk about his horses and how fat the cattle were.

"Once the beans are dry, we grade, then roast them."

Simon shot her a swift glance. His gaze had softened, and his mouth was no longer a grim slash beneath his nose.

Lise's cheeks flared hot. Their first meeting had been a disaster and she hadn't wanted a second, but when he looked at her like that, her pulse beat faster.

Simon motioned toward the factory, indicating that the boys should go ahead. He waited for

Lise and Michael to join him.

Simon's own distinctive scent engulfed her, blocking out the smoky, sweaty smell of the boys. He didn't take her arm again, but walked close to her side, the warmth emanating from his body hotter than the sun in the rarefied highlands air.

Once inside the factory, the noise was overwhelming.

The machinery clacked and jangled, the engines roared. Conveyor belts swept the coffee beans from machine to machine. Brown men, perspiration dripping from their faces, manned the electrical tangle, each scanning his own area for problems.

The group halted before a funnel spewing coffee beans into an auger below. Lise leaned closer, fascinated as the beans flowed into the spout like lava down a mountain.

The air was close. She fingered her opal, lifting it away from the dampness of her skin. A boy jostled her from behind, knocking her arm. The chain of her necklace snapped.

"No!" she cried, her belly clenching as the small stone slipped from the broken chain and flew into the spout, a pale glistening oval amongst the brown beans.

A strong brown arm pushed her to one side,

then flashed into the vat of swiftly disappearing beans. The grinding metal parts at the bottom of the auger growled menacingly.

"Simon! No!" she cried again.

Her eyes focused in horror on the fine black hairs covering Simon's skin. Seeming not to care about the metal blades biting into the beans just inches below his fingers, he plunged his arm in deeper. He reached, he grasped, then reached once more as the opal swirled down the spout as inexorably as water.

Lise's heart pounded. How could he? The opal had been her mother's and she loved it, but she refused to have anything else on her conscience. Certainly not Simon's mangled hand.

She gazed around wildly, searching for something, anything, to use as a tourniquet. If his fingers were caught, the blood would . . . Her stomach lifted, then dropped again.

She stared hard at Simon's intent face, determined not to give in to the dizziness making her body sway. If she focused on his face, kept her gaze away from his hand, perhaps, even now, she could stave off the faint.

He was like her father, the kind of man who flirted with danger, the kind of man she didn't want to know. Her father had weighed his chances, then plunged in anyway, uncaring, thinking himself invincible. And in the end . . .

For one ghastly moment, Simon's face became Frank Dawson's, his own strong features wavering into the less defined profile of her father.

"Stop!" Lise shrieked, her voice scarcely audible above the machine's roar. She grabbed Simon's arm and closed her fingers around his wrist. She wrenched frantically on his arm, desperate to pull it up and out of danger.

He turned and glared at her, then shook off her hand as easily as a bull shakes off a fly. Plunging his hand even lower, he stretched to grasp the stone. It eluded him, sliding further and further into the ever-narrowing opening.

Tears of fury blinded her. Why was he so willing to get his fingers chewed up for a few seconds of ill-considered bravado?

Well, let him. She was damned if she was going to thank him for it.

He had it! He drew forth the tiny opal, coffee beans falling like rain drops from his hands, and held the stone aloft, his eyes glowing with triumph.

The boys crowded around him, cheering. He stood head and shoulders above them, expanded somehow with success, larger than life, strong and invincible.

He extended the opal toward her, an exultant

grin blazoned across his face. She clenched her hands to her sides, her stomach lurching. He might have been hurt. He would claim he had done it for her, but she knew better.

His kind of man did it for the love of it, for the thrill of danger, the excitement of winning.

Well, she didn't want any part of it. When she made no move to take the delicate stone from his hand, his face darkened.

"Were you throwing it away, then?" he growled. "You're always touching the damn thing. I could have sworn you loved it."

The boys were as silent as wet leaves, not a crackle or rustle could be heard. The machinery roared but everyone was listening . . . waiting.

Lise's chest tightened. Simon was watching her, his eyes ominous in their stillness. She took a deep breath, her mouth dry.

"I don't want it," she said fiercely. "I didn't ask you to get it. You might have been hurt."

"So, you do care." His voice was mocking, seductive.

"You wanted to rescue it that badly, you keep it," she said from between gritted teeth.

His eyes narrowed and he stepped toward her again, holding out the opal. He filled the space in front of her, pressuring her with his nearness.

The boys began to whisper, their low voices breaking through her indecision.

She took two steps backward, stared one last time into Simon's now furious eyes, then whirled around. She pushed her way through the students and ran from the building.

Chapter Four

Lise bent at the waist, put her hands on her knees, and gulped in huge lungsful of air. The blood rushed back to her head, easing the dizzy sensation she had fought as she fled the building.

She was out of shape, that's all it was. She struggled to push away the image of Simon, but couldn't.

Damn him! She pressed her eyes more tightly shut, determined to stop the world from spinning. Sharp lines of light still pierced the darkness beneath her lids, wavering and jiggling like demented sunbeams.

It was no use. Forcing open her eyes, she straightened, her face flushed and hot. Her hand stole up her neck from habit and felt for her necklace.

Gone.

She moaned, and clamped her lips together, fighting the anger threatening to erupt. Her first reaction had been the one to trust. Keep clear of Simon. He was exactly the sort of man she'd vowed to stay away from. Aerial stunts, motor cross racing, the scar down his cheek, and now her opal.

She couldn't afford to learn to like the man, to be attracted to him. He was another like her father and she couldn't bear that kind of pain again.

Simon was the sort of man who would make her worry, and her worry would eat away at her until she became nothing, like her mother had become nothing. She had died a tiny death with every action her husband had taken, until finally she was gone.

Lise gazed numbly at the sparkling river at her feet, its continuous movement calming her. Her breathing deepened, then slowed. She glanced behind her. How had she made it down the cliff?

She couldn't remember any trail. She'd run from the building, her vision blurred by tears, then plunged into the trees, desiring simply to get away from everyone and pull herself together. Immediately, the level ground had dropped away and she'd half-fallen, half-scrambled down the cliff toward the river.

Somehow she'd have to get back up, though at the top would be Simon. She would rather stay here, where he wasn't, where it was quiet and peaceful. Even the noise from the factory was deadened by the cliff and the thick stand of trees.

The silence suddenly seemed even louder.

"Considering how to apologize?" Simon asked from behind.

She whirled. Simon towered above her, the space between them vibrating with explosive energy.

"Not for a moment." She would never admit she had been thinking of him.

A deep-throated laugh rumbled up from Simon's chest and resonated over the river. Lise took a step backward. He looked like the devil himself standing there so confidently, framed by the trees.

"What, then?" Simon asked.

It was his eyes which compelled an answer. She never lied, but perhaps a half-truth would suffice. "I was thinking of my parents."

"Missing them already?"

"They're dead," she said flatly, turning her head to hide the tears misting her eyes. She could not, would not, cry in front of this man.

A branch snapped as Simon moved toward her. She stood her ground, denying the impulse to run back up the cliff and away from this man.

Strong fingers cupped her chin. Gently, he tilted her face upward. She shut her eyes to hide her tears.

"Lise."

Her mouth went dry, as did her lips. She swept her tongue over them, knowing she couldn't stand there forever feeling him touch her skin. She opened her eyes, willing her tears to miraculously disappear.

The dark centers of his eyes were soft, filled with a sympathy needing no words. Her brow furrowed, pain hammering the inside of her forehead. With unexpected tenderness, he took hold of her and drew her to him.

She stiffened, but he didn't release her. Then her body touched his and her resistance died. She melted against him, allowing his comfort and strength to envelop her. She gave herself up to it, letting go for the first time since her father died.

When his mouth sought hers, she froze, but his lips were as gentle as the touch of a butterfly. He pulled her even closer, crushing her against his chest. His warmth penetrated her light clothing, and her hands crept around his neck, entwining themselves in the soft waves at the edge of his hairline.

He groaned, his lips hardening on hers, demanding to explore her mouth more intimately. Passion flickered hotly through her, warmth and comfort disappearing like a sigh.

She had never been kissed like this.

Breathlessly.

Endlessly.

Then, with bewildering suddenness, he thrust her away. The sound of the boys chattering and laughing on the hillside above drilled into her consciousness. She looked at him, her cheeks hot. She tried to speak, but his expression forbade it. His face had changed. He swiped the back of his hand across his forehead and stared down at her, his eyes narrowing, as though he saw or felt something he despised.

She tried again. "Simon, I—"

"Save it, sweetheart," he said curtly. "It felt good, didn't it?"

Her throat turned raw as she faced eyes like blocks of granite.

"But you don't want a repetition, do you?" His knuckles traced a line down her cheek, but his gesture held no warmth. "Neither do I."

"I don't understand," she whispered, jerking away from his touch.

"I knew you'd be trouble," he said softly, so softly, he could have been speaking to himself. His gaze drifted over her. "At least you've got your travel story now. You can go home happy." He touched her cheek again, as though he couldn't stop himself. "It would be fun to play further, but we both know how that would end. I like your aunt too much to allow that to happen."

Trembling began deep in the pit of Lise's stomach. "I've had better kisses," she lied. "But you're right, it gives me something to laugh about when I go home."

His eyes flashed a warning. She stepped backward, away from his anger. Then the corners of his mouth twitched. "Not the best you've had?" His gaze lowered to her mouth. "We may be forced to practice."

The way he said it, it was a threat. Lise's chest heaved but before she could answer, Simon took hold of her hand and half-pulled, half-dragged her through the bushes and up the hill toward the factory.

Brother Michael and the boys eyed them curiously as they emerged from the trees. Heat blazed across Lise's face. Damn Simon!

"Uncle Simon!"

An arm-churning imp bolted from the factory office and ran toward them. His hair lifted as he ran, cascading down again like a blond bowl as he skidded to a stop in front of his uncle.

"Where were you?" the boy demanded, his brown eyes fierce. "You promised Raz and I could go with you when the students came." He glanced plaintively in the direction of Michael and the boys. "Now they're all finished."

Simon rested his hand on the small boy's shoulder. "You promised me you'd get your math finished first. Is it done?"

The boy's chin sunk into his chest. "No," he mumbled, jabbing the stick he was clutching into the dirt. "Almost."

"We'll go riding together later on this afternoon," Simon said, shifting his hand to the top of the boy's head and stroking his hair. "After you're done. Just a short ride, mind. You're still recuperating."

The boy's head jerked upward and he grinned. It was as though the sun had come out. Simon smiled too, then cuffed the child gently on the shoulder, a gesture which sent the child rocketing back toward the office.

Lise chewed her inner lip. The boy had diverted his uncle's attention, but now Connor was gone. Simon moved toward Michael and spoke to him in a rapid undertone. She couldn't hear what was said, but Michael's face lit up as Connor's had done. He grabbed Simon's hand and shook it.

As though prompted by some unseen signal, the boys surged toward the truck. Michael moved with them, but Simon turned and waited for her.

His gaze burned a path through the glare of the sun and the dust kicked up by the boy's feet. Lise's legs ignored all messages from her brain to move. Michael was already opening the cab door to his truck, yet still Simon waited.

Lise slowly released the air captured in her lungs.

The sun was behind Simon, its glare obliterating the stark outline of his face and all sign of his scar. But nothing could hide the way he was staring at her, a faint smile tugging his lips.

His hands were jammed into his pockets, but she didn't need to see them to be reminded how they felt caressing her cheek, passing down her arms and settling on the small of her back.

"Lise," Michael called, pulling her gaze to him. He was poised to leave, one foot on the step of the truck. "Simon and I have a wager to discuss." His voice lilted with excitement. "I'm going to take the boys back to the school and meet the two of you at the club."

She glanced sharply at Simon. His face told her nothing.

"If you have things to discuss," she said, "just drop me at Aunt Cecile's." More time spent with Simon was unthinkable.

"It's too nice a day to spend the afternoon at home," Simon said implacably. "Your aunt wants you to get out and meet people, not hide away in a convent."

Lise stared at him, stunned. Aunt Cecile would never have said such a thing.

Michael stepped to the ground again, his face anxious, his eyes imploring her to say yes. Frowning, Lise looked again at Simon. His eyes were critical, as though he were positive she wouldn't come.

Anger rattled through her. Both men were waiting for her answer; the one hopeful, the other certain he knew what that answer would be. She tilted up her chin. Mr Simon McDowell did not know everything. "Sounds like fun," she said.

~*~

She had made a mistake.

Simon held the wheel loosely, but his body seemed coiled as tightly as a spring. Lise's leg muscles were cramped from jamming her feet onto imaginary brakes at each bend in the road.

"Can't you slow down?" she demanded, gripping the door handle, determined not to fly into Simon's arms a second time.

"We're here." He swerved the vehicle into the parking lot and braked to a stop.

Lise climbed out quickly, giving him no

chance to come around and open her door. He walked to the club house beside her, not touching her. For one irrational moment, she wished that he would.

She pressed through the doorway first, fighting the urge to lean back against his chest.

The front of the building did no justice to the décor inside. Great panels of interlocking grasses covered the walls as they would a hut in the jungle. Sturdy pieces of bamboo were lashed together to form a bar fronted by small tables and brightly cushioned wicker chairs.

Simon led the way to a table in the corner. Lise dropped into her chair with her back to the room, apprehension niggling her chest like flies around a horse on a hot summer's day. When she raised her eyes, her heart sank further.

For now there was only Simon.

He placed his hands on the table before her, palms upward. "Peace," he said, his mouth melting into a lopsided grin. "We should be able to manage an hour or two without rubbing each other the wrong way."

She doubted it. But when he looked at her like that, his eyes smiling and meaning it, his face turned appealingly toward hers, it was impossible to say no.

She sighed. "We can try."

"Good. Would you like a beer? It's important to drink plenty of liquids in the tropics."

At her nod, he motioned to the waiter. Within minutes, their drinks were in front of them. Lise held her glass against her forehead, cooling the perspiration forming there.

At last, reluctantly, she met Simon's eyes.

"So," she said. "What kind of wager did you make with Michael?"

He grinned, looking momentarily exactly like Connor.

"Michael and I are both entered in the Club's annual horse race," he said, leaning across the table toward Lise. "We've put a small wager on the outcome."

"What kind of wager?"

"If I win, he's promised to spend his Saturdays for the next school term teaching the laborer's children how to read and write."

"Don't they already go to school?"

Simon shook his head. "Only a fraction of the children in the highlands go to elementary school. There aren't enough places or money for the rest. Plantation workers' children, no hope!"

"It's nice of you," Lise said softly.

He shrugged her compliment away.

"Michael would probably have done it for you regardless."

"Sure he would, but where's the fun in that?"

She smiled at his outraged expression. "And if you lose?"

"I find someone to man the mission station's haus sik."

Her brow creased. "What's that?"

"First aid post." He leaned toward her. "I was thinking of you."

"Wha . . .t!" she spluttered.

"You say you're not just a tourist." He reached across the table and ran his fingers over her hand. "Prove it."

"You didn't promise my services, did you?" She yanked her hand away. She couldn't deal with patients again. The mere thought made her feel ill. Students, laborers, villagers, all trusting her. She shuddered.

"It's hardly a big thing," Simon said, lazily lifting his hand. "Working in the haus sik isn't difficult. It's simply a matter of applying a few bandages and ointments. You don't have to be a nurse."

"You have no right to make promises on my behalf!"

His eyes narrowed.

"I won't do it." She had promised herself when she left the States that she needn't have anything more to do with patients.

"I should have guessed," Simon said, pushing his chair back. "I did guess, but took a chance I was wrong. Can't bear to become involved, can you? Can't even put on the odd bandage! You'd rather take pictures of the natives than help where it's needed."

His contempt lashed at her. She stared numbly at her hands. She'd heaped the same sort of scorn on herself many times in the last few months, but it hadn't made any difference.

"Here you are," Michael said, approaching them from behind Lise.

She glanced up, watching as Michael pulled up a chair and beckoned to the waiter for a drink.

"Did you tell her about it, Simon?" Michael asked eagerly.

Simon nodded, his lips tightening. "Lise doesn't think much of the idea."

Her cheeks flooded with heat. Michael's astonished glance drowned her in shame and guilt.

Simon leaned forward again, his gaze calculating. "Perhaps if we sweeten the pot a little, give Miss Dawson an incentive." He became silent then, as if searching for her Achilles heel.

She hadn't realized until that instant that she was holding her breath.

"If Brother Michael wins," Simon said at last, "I'll throw in a computer and printer for the school." He glanced inquiringly at Michael. "You don't have one, do you, Michael?"

"Have one?" he breathed. "We barely have books." His grey eyes came alive with desire.

Lise's stomach churned. She had to say no, but Simon had made it impossible. His triumphant eyes reflected her defeat back at her.

"I'll do it," she said finally.

"What a wager," Michael said, thumping Simon on the shoulder. "No matter who loses, the people win. Even the bishop can't object to that."

Then Michael turned to her. "Thank you, Lise. It'll be a busman's holiday, but it's very good of you. We've always had to make do with one of the brothers manning the first aid station, but to actually have a qualified doctor!"

Chapter Five

"A doctor!" The words seemed to clang from his own lips like a death knell, jarring Simon's ears, hurting his head.

Lise's chest rose as if from a swift breath.

Heat swept his cheeks at the sight of her eyes, so enormous, so luminous . . . so guilty.

"A doctor," he said again, dully this time, thinking, somehow, that if he kept his tone even, the word would transform, become something else. That she'd become something else. That she wouldn't be what Marion had been, a doctor who wouldn't doctor.

He grabbed her wrist when she made a move to stand.

"Why?" he demanded, the heat fleeing his body, leaving it cold. His words were cold, too, like water dripping off a glacier. "Why did you lie to me?"

Why did any woman?

Why had Marion?

His ex-wife had worked to her own agenda. As Lise obviously did, too.

She ceased her attempt to stand and

remained seated, saying nothing with her lips. She must think she was safe, but her eyes told him everything.

He swallowed hard, forcing away the pain piercing his body, horrified at how deeply Lise had gotten under his skin. He'd been sure the agony allocated for his lifetime was finished, that nothing could hurt him again as Marion had done. He had been wrong.

"I told you how desperate we were for medical staff!"

He stopped, even now praying Lise would interrupt, praying she would give him some logical reason for her lies.

Still she said nothing, but her lower lip shook.

Against all reason, against all that was rational, he had a sudden urge to touch her, to soothe her, to stop her trembling. It took all the will he had, all the remembered hurt from eight years past, to stop the impulse.

"You didn't want to be bothered," he said instead, his heart hardening. Like Marion hadn't wanted to be bothered. The haus sik was beneath her, Marion had said. She was a doctor, not a first-aid attendant. She had no interest in dispensing bandages with all the case histories she had left to compile.

The color had drained from Lise's face. Her

gaze seemed glued to his, as though she could no more look away than he.

"Afraid it might interfere with your career plans?" he asked, not even trying to keep the bitterness from his voice.

"Hold on, Simon," Michael said. "Lise hasn't had time to tell us anything. Besides, she barely knows us."

"No time?" Simon repeated. Barely knew them? It felt as though he had known her forever. "Is that why you didn't tell us, Dr. Dawson?"

Her color swept back, reddening her cheeks. With what seemed an enormous effort of will, she met his gaze.

"Well?" he demanded.

Perspiration shone on her forehead. Her eyes glazed over as though her thoughts had turned inward. She shuddered, her slim arms quivering as if from cold. Then she looked at him again, her eyes refocusing and her lips tightening.

"Yes, I'm a doctor," she said. "But what makes you think I should have told you?" Her voice trembled on her last words. "I assumed we'd never meet again."

"You think it's all right to lie to strangers?" he demanded, scorn twisting his lips. "I told you why I'd been to Australia. I told you how difficult it was to find someone good to practice in New Guinea." The heat from his words seemed to scorch his lips. "What stopped you from telling me you were a doctor?" For an instant, he wished he could close off his ears.

"I didn't say anything because—" Her chest rose, then fell again rapidly.

If he didn't hear her answer, the pain might disappear.

"—I don't intend to practice."

A thundering erupted in his head, threatening to obliterate all sound.

"I have a research job beginning in three months."

"Research!" He pressed his eyes shut, but nothing could arrest the image of Marion standing before him in her elegant black dress, pearls gleaming coldly around her neck, informing him he could keep New Guinea, she was going back to Sydney.

He opened his eyes and stared hard at Lise. "Locked up in some dry-as-dust room proving old men's theories!"

Her cheeks burned. "I have my own theories."

"No doubt you do. But a woman like you, a warm woman, a passionate woman, shouldn't be working with cold facts and figures and . . . and theories." Her dark eyes seemed blue all at once.

As Marion's had been blue.

"There's no money in research." His jaw felt stiff, making it difficult to speak. "Unless it's prestige you're after."

He'd told Marion they would both move, but very calmly, she had said no. It was the calmness that had hurt the most. As though she didn't care at all. As though even their lust for each other had meant nothing.

For he knew now it hadn't been love. Not like his parents had loved. A forever and always kind of love.

Her field research into malaria was finished, Marion had said. She had all the data she needed. She would complete her project in Sydney, somewhere more civilized, somewhere her paper would get the publicity it deserved.

Her career would be made, she had said with a satisfied smile. That smile had turned his heart to ice, as it did again now just thinking about it. Desperately, he wrenched his attention back to Lise.

Her color had disappeared again, washing away like the morning tide, but her shoulders were straight.

"It really doesn't matter what I'm after." Her chin rose higher. "It's no business of yours."

"That's where you're wrong." Relentlessly, he

held her gaze. "You've promised to take part in the wager. I intend to see you honor that promise."

"That won't be necessary." Lise struggled to keep her voice dignified. "When I make a promise, I keep it."

By a thin thread, she hung onto her courage. Somehow, her hand was still clasped in Simon's. She tugged it loose.

He let her go, as though glad to be rid of her. She rubbed her squeezed fingers, forcing the circulation to begin flowing again. She stood.

"The two of you can discuss your wager on your own. I'm going to look around."

She moved away, cutting short Michael's protest. Simon didn't bother to object. When she glanced over her shoulder, he had lounged back into his seat, his gaze following her.

She forced herself not to hurry, weaving between the other tables, people's faces a blur. She swerved around the bar and the men crowding up to it, then pushed through the door to the ladies room.

Once inside, she expelled her breath in a fierce gust. Raising one hand to her hair, she yanked her tangled curls loose from the elastic band holding them, propped her hands on the edge of the sink and shut her eyes.

"Hello."

Lise groaned. She hadn't noticed anyone else in the room. Pushing herself away from the sink, she opened her eyes.

A woman emerged from one of the change cubicles, her honey blonde hair cascading lightly over the top of a hot-pink bikini.

"I'm Sylvie," the woman said, her lips parting in a smile. She faced a mirror, took a comb from her bag, and pulled it through her hair.

"Lise Dawson," Lise said, working hard to keep her voice steady.

The other woman glanced at her from beneath long, pale lashes. Then her blue eyes turned shrewd. "Are you all right? I saw you come in with Simon. Don't tell me he's broken your heart already."

Lise stared at her. "What do you mean?"

Sylvie shrugged. "Every woman in the valley has been in love with him at one point or other." She laughed. "Including me!"

Lise couldn't imagine a more difficult man to love. Then, unbidden, the memory surfaced of his arms around her body. How they'd felt. Their warmth. Their strength.

"I'm not in love with him," she denied.

"Good," Sylvie said, smiling, though her brows rose. "Then you won't get hurt.

"I'm surprised he's not married." The comment fell from Lise's lips before she could stop it. It wasn't surprising at all. Hard to imagine Simon a half-of-a-whole.

Sylvie frowned. "He was. A woman from Sydney. Didn't he tell you?"

"No." Lise answered. "No reason why he should." She hesitated, but couldn't stop herself asking, "What happened?"

Sylvie carefully applied a fuchsia lip gloss. "She left," Sylvie said, blotting her lips with a tissue.

Lise's breath escaped. She captured another one. "Why didn't he go with her?"

Sylvie raised one slim shoulder. "Perhaps he didn't want to." She pursed her lips. "Nobody dared ask." She turned back to the mirror and gathered her hair into a pony tail. "Going swimming?" she asked, tying her pony tail with a white ribbon.

If only a swim could blot out the day, the bet Simon had made with Michael, the way Simon had looked at her, his face filled with contempt, the things Sylvie had told her . . .

Lise sighed. It wasn't just the day she wanted to forget. It was the last few months. That terrible moment when her father had fallen from his horse, his head smashing hard on the rock, and the blood, all that blood she couldn't stop.

Ridiculous to imagine she could escape into forgetfulness. She had fought her fears minute by minute to get through the days, fought the urge to confess to patients, I can't do it. I can't make you well. Best get someone else.

She licked her dry lips. She could never explain any of that to anyone. And now, if Michael won, she'd have to work with patients, the one thing she had sworn she would never do again.

"I'll be here for the afternoon," Sylvie continued, smiling at herself in the mirror, seeming satisfied at last with her reflection. "You can join me if you like."

"I don't have a suit," Lise said.

"No problem. I always keep a spare in my locker."

Sylvie turned, pulled open a metal door and rummaged through a heap of shorts, tops, and tennis shoes. "Got it!" she exclaimed, holding up a black one-piece. She tossed it to Lise and headed for the door. "I'll wait for you outside."

Lise held the suit up in front of her. Not a bikini, thank heavens! But almost as revealing. Quickly, she donned it, tugging at the fabric above the high-cut legs, trying to make it cover her body better. It simply plunged lower between her breasts.

She grimaced at her reflection in the mirror, a rush of nerves bombarding her chest. Hardening her resolve, she clutched one of Sylvie's towels to her front and stepped through the door to the pool patio. No sign of Simon, thank goodness.

"Lise," Sylvie called. "Over here!" The blonde woman shifted her iced drink to her other hand and pulled Lise into a circle of smiling faces. "This is Jim Mathews," she said, grinning cheekily as she touched the arm of the handsome blond man on her other side. "I have to introduce him first or he'll sulk."

Lise chuckled, the butterflies in her chest gliding to a halt.

"And this is Sue, and Dave. Lise is here all the way from…" Sylvie glanced at her.

"The States."

"Must be quite a change coming here!" Sue exclaimed.

"It is," Lise answered. More than she had expected.

"Enjoy it while you can." Sue grinned. "If you stay long enough one of these fellows will convince you to marry him and you'll be wedded to the bush for life." She winked at Dave.

A shadow fell over Lise. She glanced over her

shoulder and saw Simon coming through the patio door. Heart thumping, she turned back to the group.

"A fate worse than death!" Jim teased. Then he held out his hand. "Come on Lise, let's go for a dip before Sue scares you off home on the next plane."

Lise nodded, chancing another glance over her shoulder. Simon was gone. Her pulse slowed. She followed Jim to the edge of the pool and dove in before him. She longed to stay below forever, no one talking, no one watching, but unable to hold her breath any longer, she shot to the surface.

"I thought you had drowned," Jim said, treading water beside her.

She shook her head, endeavoring to smile.

"What do you think of New Guinea so far?"

Impossible to think of the country when the memory of Simon's lips descending toward her own played over and over in her mind, like a film snagged in one spot. She slipped below the surface of the water once more, needing to obliterate the image. Jim grabbed her hand and pulled her back up.

"You look as though you've seen a ghost," he said, examining her face.

"No ghost."

"No tribal fights, either? No sorcery?"

"Tribal fights? Sorcery?" She frowned.

"We have them all in New Guinea," he proclaimed cheerfully, pulling her toward him. "Better stick close to me. I'll keep you safe." He put his hands around her waist.

It was too intimate, too familiar.

"Enjoying yourselves?"

Simon's words hovered over Lise's head like a cap of ice. Jim's grip tightened, pulling her closer. Lise raised one hand to her eyes, blinded by Simon's outline against the glare of the sun. He had changed into swim trunks and he towered above her.

"Yes," she muttered. Damn the man. And damn Jim, too, holding her in such a ridiculous clinch. She wiggled free.

"Coming in?" she asked Simon, intent on keeping her voice light.

"Not now." He walked toward Sylvie and her friends, his shoulders as taut as his voice. He could see the pool from where he now sat under the shade of a bamboo umbrella.

"Lap time," she said to Jim, her voice brittle with strain. She felt uncomfortably like a butterfly on a pin as she pushed off against the side and surged down the pool, desperate to wash away the tension, the memory of the riverside that morning and the feel of Simon's hands on her body.

The movement wasn't helping. She swam harder, stroking back and forth across the pool, until finally she stopped, exhausted. Holding onto the pool's edge, she gulped a large breath of air.

Jim swam up beside her and hoisted himself out. "Like a drink?"

She nodded, then shut her eyes and raised her face to the sun. Its heat burned the water off her skin, but still she felt chilled.

"I didn't think you knew how to swim," Simon said, his voice as cold as her thoughts, "given the way the river frightened you before."

Lise opened her eyes. She had known he was beside her before he had even spoken. The heat of his body seemed to penetrate the water rippling around her.

"That river was dangerous. It was terrifying."

"Dangerous, maybe. But terrifying?" He shook his head. "Depends on how you approach it."

"The only one way to approach it is to stay out of it."

He shrugged. "Sometimes you don't have a choice." Then, he smiled. "Where did you learn to swim like that?"

"Cold Montana lakes," Lise said, shivering, trying to ignore how she felt with him so near. "You swim fast or you freeze . . . and I don't like to be cold."

"You're not cold." He was very close to her now. His eyes had darkened to the ebony of a tropical night with no lights to be seen but the stars.

Her lips parted. She could get lost in those eyes . . . sucked into them . . . drowned.

"That's why I don't understand," he said, his voice turning hard, shattering the spell his eyes had created.

She stared across at him, her heart pounding.

"You said you'd run the haus sik if Michael wins, but why don't you want to? What are you afraid of?"

Everything. She was afraid of everything.

"Nothing," she said, her voice sounding too loud to her ears. "I'm not afraid of anything." She had said it convincingly. She knew she had. Why didn't he look convinced?

She turned her head to escape his probing gaze but he cupped her chin in his hand and forced her to face him. "What is it, Lise?"

She regarded him stonily.

"I'm going to find out, you know."

He would. He was that kind of man. He

wouldn't let it drop until he knew. In a way, it would be a relief to tell someone. Her shoulders sagged. But what good would it do? The pain and shame would never go away and she couldn't bear his pity. Maybe if she told him part of it. Maybe that would satisfy him.

"It's—" She took a breath. "—not a very interesting story."

"Let me be the judge of that."

"I simply discovered I don't enjoy working with patients."

"I don't believe that."

"It's true. You can believe it or not. I don't care."

His eyes turned as hard as black diamonds. "When did you discover this?"

"After my residency." The lie lodged in her throat. "That's why I decided to take the job in research."

He clutched the side of the pool, his knuckles turning white.

She was sweating now. Perspiration gathered on her forehead and streamed down her hairline to her neck. "A good doctor has to have the confidence of her patients," she exclaimed, desperate to make him see. "I don't have that."

He didn't believe her. She could see it in his eyes. "I can't work with patients," she repeated.

"Then it's time you learned differently." He ducked beneath the surface, then came up again, shaking his head and releasing the drops in a silvery spray.

"What do you mean?"

"If your problem is as you say." His face was tight with suspicion. "If you simply lack confidence—"

There was nothing simple about it.

"—then it's easy to fix."

She almost believed him. He seemed strong enough to fix anything. But not this. No one could fix this.

"When you fall off a horse—"

She could see her father falling . . . falling. She moaned and shut her eyes. Simon touched her arm and she opened them again.

"—you get right back on."

"Maybe you do," she muttered bitterly.

"You can too!" His face was serious, but his lips spread into a smile. "I'll even give you a boost."

"And if I don't want to?"

He shrugged. "If Michael wins, you'll have to."

Panic coursed through her.

"Here's your drink, Lise."

She blinked at the sound of Jim's voice.

"Thanks Jim," she said weakly. She put her palms on the cement, preparing to pull herself out. Suddenly, Simon's hands were around her waist. He boosted her onto the edge of the pool as though she weighed nothing. She scrambled to her feet.

He followed her, water falling off his bronzed back in glistening drops. "The club's horse race dinner and dance is coming up in a couple of days," he said, looking only at her. "I'm having a barbecue the night before."

She didn't want to go, couldn't go.

"I'd like you to come."

Especially to his house.

"Too late, McDowell," Jim said.

Lise glanced at him, startled.

Jim placed his arm across her shoulders. "Lise is coming to the club with me that night for a drink."

Simon frowned, not shifting his gaze from Lise.

Lise dared not look at Jim, dared not let Simon see he had lied. Heat blazed across her cheeks.

"I see," Simon said. He took a few steps away, then glanced over his shoulder. "Plenty to drink at my house."

He smiled enigmatically. "See you both there."

Chapter Six

Reluctantly, Lise faced the rambling house before her. It's ornate front door loomed, challenging her to knock. She raised her hand.

What if Simon answered the door himself?

Her arm dropped back to her side. She wasn't sure she was ready to face him. The muffled roar of a motorbike sounded behind her. She spun around. The bike and its rider raced toward her along the path from the factory, gravel spraying up as the bike slammed to a stop.

The rider, an Akubra hat pulled low over his face, swung one lean leg over the seat, then slapped his hands hard against his jeans. Grey dust from the drive floated up where his hands hit.

She would have known those shoulders anywhere.

Simon smiled slowly as the dust settled. "Glad you could make it, Lise."

She frowned at the bike, then her frown deepened as she glanced at the scar on his face. "You still ride that thing?"

His smile froze. "Of course."

"Are you crazy?"

"Sometimes."

"It's dangerous." Her voice wobbled. She steadied herself. "You might get hurt."

A glint appeared in his eyes as he leaned forward. "It sounds as though you care," he said softly.

"Of course I care," she snapped. "I'm a physician."

The glint disappeared. He parked the bike next to the house and brushed past her. "You're not my physician," he growled over his shoulder. "Or my mother." He turned to face her. "Or my wife. So you don't have a say, do you?"

Heat scalded her cheeks.

He folded his arms across his chest.

She held her breath.

He stared at her long and hard, then unexpectedly, he held out his hand.

She didn't take it.

"Come on," was all he said. "I'll take you around back to meet the other guests." Ruefully, he glanced at his jeans. "Then I'll have to go change. There was a problem at the factory."

Lise let out her breath. Why had she come? "Don't worry about me. I'll find my own way or wait for Jim."

"He's here?"

"Just parking the car."

Simon stepped closer, his eyes impossibly dark. She felt dwarfed next to him. Something vibrated in the air between them, intensifying as he drew closer. It was impossible to retreat, to advance, to go anywhere at all.

He gazed down at her, then reached for her hand again.

"Come on," he urged.

She yanked her fingers from his grasp.

He looked amused. "It gives me a chance to work on you," he explained, then headed off along the side of the house, not waiting to see if she followed.

"Work on me?" she asked, irritated when her feet moved her along after him.

"You know you'll be wasted in research."

She gaped at him, hurrying to keep pace.

"You'd be far better off staying in New Guinea and working in the new hospital." He held himself stiffly as though his suggestion were a test he expected her to fail.

Her throat tightened.

"The people here need you."

"I told you, I don't want to work with patients."

His face grew grim, his eyes darkening to the

color of slate as he scowled down at her. "You'll change your mind."

Goosebumps rose on her arms. He sounded so sure. But he couldn't know.

Blindly, she turned and moved back in the direction she had come. Before she had gone two strides, he was beside her. He caught her by the shoulder and spun her around to face him.

"It's something else, isn't it?" he demanded, his eyes seeming determined to make her say it was.

She stared back at him, numb.

"Whatever it is you're running from, you're not going to beat it without a fight."

Her lips quivered. "Who says I want to beat it?"

His eyes burned. "I do. You've got what it takes."

His words cast a glow, warming her, calming her.

"Simon—" She wanted to say more but couldn't. She swallowed again and looked away. She couldn't talk about it. Not now. Not ever.

She moved forward, Simon behind her. They turned the corner of the house and a broad expanse of lawn, brilliant green in the sunlight, spread out before her. Its brightness filtered through the tears forming in her eyes.

"There are a lot of people here," she said, her voice trembling. She fought to steady it. "I wouldn't have guessed there were this many expatriates in the area."

Simon came up beside her. He glanced toward his guests and frowned, opened his mouth to speak, then seemed to change his mind. He tugged his hat down over his brow.

"The Waghi Valley is the best coffee and tea growing valley in New Guinea. Add up the plantation owners, teachers, health workers, business people and government agents and you've got a lot of people."

"Most of them seem to be here."

He ran a hand lovingly over the red wood of the wall beside him. "This house was built for parties." He shrugged. "In New Guinea, there aren't many places to go. Few movies, except at the club, few dances, few restaurants." He seemed to be gauging her reaction. "You make your own fun or there is none."

"Don't you ever want to get away?"

"Seldom," he said, his face darkening. He looked across the lawns and beyond, to the acres of coffee surrounding them. "I never get tired of this." Then, he faced her again. "But when I want a change of scenery, I fly to one of the islands on the coast."

"And Australia?"

A muscle twitched below his right temple. "Nothing I want there."

His ex-wife was Australian and from the way his face shuttered, it was obvious she had hurt him. Why hadn't he followed her if he loved her that much? Her gaze traced the set line of his lips. He was too damn stubborn, that's why.

Simon glanced toward the drive. "Here comes Mathews," he drawled. His gaze flickered over her face as though searching for something, then he raised his hand and touched her cheek.

The sandpapery roughness of his fingers felt good. Suddenly, she longed for him to touch her again.

"Don't forget what I said," he reminded her before his hand dropped away.

If only she could.

~*~

There was no sign now of dust on Simon. His linen pants were tropical white. His inky hair, waving softly above his collar, contrasted sharply with the scarlet of his cotton shirt. Lise jerked her gaze away and tried to pay attention to what Jim was saying. Aunt Cecile's gusty laugh sounded from somewhere behind. Lise frowned. What would her aunt think if she knew how Simon made her feel?

Aunt Cecile would probably think it was wonderful.

But it wasn't.

"I'm sure Lise would find sorcerers fascinating. Isn't that right, Lise?"

"Pardon?" They were all staring at her.

"You were a million miles away," Jim accused.

Brother Michael looked worried. "Are you all right? It's pretty hot out here."

"Sorry. You were saying something about sorcery?"

Brother Michael nodded. "We had an incident last week at the high school. I'd just made my rounds of the boys' dormitories when one of the students ran up to me, eyes rolling, obviously terrified. Stuttering with fear, he said one of the Enga boys had become possessed with spirits."

Simon's dark head was just in her line of vision. If she shifted her feet slightly . . .

"His wantoks, people of the same language group," Michael explained, "were taking him down to the river to douse him in river water, a sure cure for spirit possession, when he escaped."

Was there a cure for the trembling that originated somewhere in the region of her knees when Simon looked at her . . .

"I heard a roar from near the river and ran down to investigate."

. . . or the roaring in her ears when he spoke?

"The boarders, nearly two hundred boys, surged around and past me, shouting. 'What is it?' I hollered. 'There,' they cried, pointing upward. They said the Enga boy was flying from tree top to tree top."

Her pulse raced so hard whenever Simon touched her, it set her body to flight. "And?" she managed to ask, dragging her attention back to the story.

Michael shrugged. "I saw nothing."

"And the boy?"

"He got better. I left him in the care of his wantoks. If I interfered and something went wrong, I'd be held responsible, along with the school." He grimaced. "A few years back, a tribe attacked the school with their spears and bows and arrows because one of their boys got sick while attending classes. They reckoned it was sorcery. They ran through the school grounds brandishing their weapons, then forced all the staff into the office building while they negotiated compensation with the headmaster."

And Simon wanted her to take over the haus sik! If she made a mistake on one of the boys she'd not only feel terrible but the whole tribe would be after her as well.

Simon didn't look as though he had a care in the world. His head was thrown back and he was laughing.

Her chest tight with tension, Lise turned back to the others. Michael was talking to Aunt Cecile now, and Jim had wandered off to get everyone a drink. If she could just slip away, go off by herself so she could think. If she could just train herself not to think.

She edged to the far side of the garden, then passed behind a hedge. The exquisite perfume of roses wafted forward to meet her.

Suddenly, the tangy scent of Simon's aftershave mingled with the smell of the roses.

"There you are."

She whirled at the sound of Simon's voice.

"Thinking about what I said? About staying on and working here?"

"No!" she exclaimed, then wished she had answered differently. Better he thought that than know she was thinking of him.

He scrutinized her face. "Or did you have something else on your mind?"

She repeated the denial.

He laughed, a contagious chuckle beguiling her to join him. "Never mind. You'll change your mind." He touched her shoulder with his hand. He seemed to need to touch her as much as she needed to be touched. "I'll change it for you at the horse race!"

"I'm not going."

"Or at the dinner and dance afterwards."

"I'm not going."

"You're going with me."

"I don't recall you asking."

"Come with me, Lise."

"Horse racing is dangerous. It's bad enough people do it, without me having to watch." She couldn't go with him. She couldn't bear it if something happened, if Simon's horse threw him, if Simon fell like her father had fallen and never got up again.

Simon's fingers clamped firmly onto her shoulders. "You have to come with me."

"Why?" She stared into his eyes. They were so clear, so luminous, so suddenly . . . vulnerable. A shiver trickled down her spine. His fingers trailed across her shoulder, pausing at her ear. Her breathing all but ceased.

"I want to dance with you, show you what you're missing with all this cautiousness," he whispered, continuing his exploration along the back of her neck.

"I . . . I . . ." His gaze befuddled her. Surely,

he could hear her heart pounding. A movement glimpsed through the hedge, a turquoise flash and the shimmer of Sylvie's honey-colored hair cleared her head.

"Why me," Lise demanded, her voice low and fierce. "From what I understand, there are plenty of other women willing to go with you."

He froze. "Who told you that?"

"Does it matter?"

"Not to me," he said, his lips stiff.

But it did matter, she realized suddenly, watching him.

"And it shouldn't matter to you either," he continued, his face darkening.

And then he kissed her. His lips descended slowly. She knew she should resist, that his kiss could only bring her pain, but there was an inevitableness about it that made turning away impossible.

His mouth scorched hers, igniting an answering flame. Her lips opened beneath his probing tongue, welcoming him unhindered into the moist recess behind.

He crushed her to him, her breasts flattening against his chest. Her silken dress provided no shelter from his strength, from his maleness.

"Masta Simon."

Her body melted into his. Liquid fire flowed

through her veins. She longed for the kiss to last forever.

"Masta Simon!" The voice was more urgent now.

Simon groaned.

There was no forever. There was only this moment.

A low growl emanated from the back of Simon's throat. First his lips, then his body, retreated. Lise struggled to breathe, struggled to return to the rose garden from the paradise in which she'd been.

"What is it, John?" Simon demanded impatiently, his gaze continuing to hold hers.

"Hos bilong yu i sik."

"What?" His attention snapped to his employee. Simon listened carefully as John spoke, then turned back to Lise.

"I've got to go," he said, his hand sweeping the length of her back. "You are coming with me to the dance." He said it as a promise, not a demand.

She breathed in deeply and watched him disappear behind the hedge. When he kissed her like that, she could deny him nothing.

"Hello."

She hadn't seen the small boy approach. "Hello," she echoed back, staring down into his solemn face.

"You're Miss Dawson, aren't you?"

"That's right."

"I'm Connor."

"I know," she said. "I saw you the other day. Nice hat." She reached forward, unable to resist touching the soft felt of the white cowboy hat perched jauntily on top of his head.

His face lit up. "Uncle Simon got it for me in Sydney." Connor looked at her speculatively. "My uncle said you're from the United States. Do you know any cowboys?"

"My father was a cowboy," she said, smiling. "All the men working on our ranch were cowboys."

"Really!" he said, his face glowing. Then, he frowned. "So why are you sad? If I knew a cowboy, I'd never be sad."

"Well—"

"I expect it's Uncle Simon." Connor's eyes grew sympathetic. "Was he mad? He gets mad sometimes. But he doesn't mean it." The boy's voice was earnest, his pixie face intent. "He told me so. It just means he loves me and doesn't want me to hurt myself."

"Oh," Lise said faintly.

Connor's brown eyes grew serious. "He must really love you, Miss Dawson."

Chapter Seven

"Anything goes on race day,' Aunt Cecile had said, and she was right.

No two people were dressed alike. As though it were Ascot, most of the women had chosen to wear clothes wildly unsuitable for walking about in a rough field in the wilds of New Guinea. Lise gazed bemusedly at the flowered dresses, skimpy sandals and wide-brimmed hats. There was even a woman carrying a parasol.

She smoothed the front of her skirt. Aunt Cecile had produced the perfect outfit for her, a dark grey linen riding skirt belonging years ago to Lise's grandmother. Cinched tightly at Lise's waist with a thin black belt, the full skirt fell well below her knees. It swirled around the tops of suede riding boots which clung snugly to the curve of her legs. She felt pleasurably unlike herself, as though she were playing dress up for the day.

The only thing missing was her opal. She touched the bare spot on her neck where her scarlet silk shirt opened to reveal her throat. Gone. Gone forever. For she certainly was not about to ask Simon for it back.

Simon came up beside her. Her pulse quickened and the palms of her hands grew damp. She captured her bottom lip between her teeth, disconcerted at how her body reacted to his presence.

A certain chemistry, such as she had never studied in medical school, reverberated between them. But that was all it was: chemistry. She could no more get involved with a man like Simon McDowell than work as a physician.

He wasn't even looking at her. He was eyeing the track, instead, examining the curves. Pursing his lips, he yanked his hat lower.

He was looking forward to the race, while she could only imagine, far too vividly, the horses charging by in a mile-crunching pack, a single mistake sure to spill the lot of them. Apprehension squeezed Lise's chest. She turned away, not wanting to look at the track even now when it was empty.

Connor raced past with some other little boys, barely slowing enough to wave. When Simon moved toward the temporary bar, Lise trailed along with him, accepting the cold glass of champagne he offered, trying to ignore her awareness of the way he stood, the way he moved, the nuances of expression crossing his face. She failed.

He touched her hand, his fingers lingering long enough to bring heat to her cheeks, long enough to make her heart skip a beat.

"When do you race?" she asked, pulling her hand away.

He licked a drop of champagne from his lips. "Not until later." He handed her a program. "There'll be six heats. The winner from each heat races in the grand finale."

She scanned the program, running her finger down the fine print. Brother Michael was in the first heat, Jim in the third and Simon in the fourth. Her hair prickled along her neckline. So many heats. So many chances for something to go wrong.

She handed the program back and accompanied Simon toward the roped-off track. The mission airstrip ran down the middle of it. The first group of horses were already at the starting line. Michael was behind the other competitors, desperately attempting to hold his mare steady.

CRACK!

Lise jumped at the sound of the starting pistol, adrenalin surging through her, startling her more than the gunshot itself. This was only the first race. She would never be able to endure an entire afternoon.

Her fingers clenched and unclenched as she watched Brother Michael. His horse bucked, then lunged, then galloped to the head of the pack and on to victory. Lise sighed, smiling at Michael as he rode past them on his way to the winner's circle.

She turned to Simon. He was smiling, too. At her. A warm feeling began somewhere deep within and exploded outward through her chest. Tentatively, she smiled again, at Simon this time, trying to convince herself that what she felt was relief Michael was safe.

"You see," Simon said, his voice rippling through her consciousness like sunshine on a cloudy day. "That wasn't so bad. They had a good race, nobody got hurt, and a few lucky people even made some money." A dimple flashed deep on his cheek. "I, unfortunately, wasn't one of them." He caught hold of her fingers. "Admit it," he challenged. "You enjoyed it."

"I wouldn't bet on that if I were you!" she said, feeling calmed by his words, insulated by his warmth.

"I'll take my chances." He glanced over her shoulder. "Good race, Brother! Where did you get a horse that fast?"

"A well-guarded secret," Michael replied,

drawing up beside them. He proudly stroked his mare's neck. "To tell you the truth, I wasn't sure she'd behave herself long enough to finish the race."

"I wouldn't count on winning the final heat."

"We'll see." Michael glanced toward the heavens and grinned. "Don't forget, I have friends in high places."

A bell rang and he looked over his shoulder. "Got to go. Jim's heat is about to start." He pressed his heels into his mare's sides and urged her off the track.

Lise leaned against the fence in front of her and stared toward the starting line. A guilty heat swept her face as she watched Jim maneuver his dappled grey gelding into position on the inside rail. He looked good on a horse, but . . . She turned away. It wasn't fair to compare Jim to Simon. It wasn't as though Jim lacked dash or grace.

He didn't. But he did lack something Simon most definitely had. She wasn't even sure if she could describe what it was. She simply knew that when she was with Simon, even when he infuriated her beyond bearing, she felt alive.

Simon touched her shoulder, startling her. "Pleased Jim won?" he asked.

She gazed wildly toward the finish line.

"Won?" She hadn't even seen him start. "Did he?"

"What were you doing?" Simon demanded incredulously. "Shutting your eyes again?" He scrutinized her face. "Or were you thinking about me?"

"Certainly not!" She struggled to put enough indignation in her voice to convince him. "Conceited man," she accused, suddenly afraid of his ability to see right through her.

He smiled, a private, knowing smile, then leaned forward and kissed her on the cheek. The caress was so casual, so unexpected, there was no time to block the desire flaming her face. She turned away, not wanting Simon to see what her face must reveal.

"So this is where you've been hiding," Jim exclaimed.

"Scarcely hiding," Lise murmured, relieved at the interruption.

"Good timing, Mathews," Simon said dryly. "I want you to take care of Lise while I run my heat."

"I don't need taking care of," she flashed.

"Maybe not." He regarded her thoughtfully, then headed toward the starting gate where his bossboy John held his horse. "Cheer for me," he commanded over his shoulder.

Annoyed, she turned her back on him.

"More champagne, Lise?" Jim asked. "To celebrate?"

She nodded and he went off to get it. Thank heavens, he hadn't waited for her to comment on his race!

"Miss Dawson! Miss Dawson!" Connor yelled, racing toward her. "There you are!" He peeped up at her through his too-long fringe. "I've been looking for you."

"Do you need something?"

"Uncle Simon said to watch the race with you," he whispered importantly. He peered behind Lise as though searching for someone. "He said to make sure Mr. Mathews behaves himself."

Lise choked on her drink.

"What did he mean by that?" Connor asked, his dark eyes curious.

"I can't imagine," she answered, glaring in the general direction of the starting gate, searching for Simon. He wasn't there. She scanned the riders clustered around the gate, then saw him. He was ready for his race. His long legs were bent, his knees ready to squeeze inward when the starting whistle blew. His broad shoulders were taut, his arms deceptively slack. He shifted his weight in the saddle, the horse beneath him appearing ready, too, yet as composed as its master. Simon turned his head once, his gaze sweeping the crowd.

Lise's mouth turned dry. She was positive, all at once, that he was searching for her.

The pistol cracked.

In one instant the horses were still, in the next, they were a churning mass of legs and hooves. But within moments, it was over. Simon's mount tore across the finish line well in advance of the others, assuring him a place in the final heat.

"Hurray! Hurray! Well done, Uncle Simon!" Connor yelled, jumping up and down with unabashed enthusiasm.

"I'll see you later, Miss Dawson. I'm going to the winner's circle." He trotted off, beaming.

Jim arrived back and handed Lise a glass of champagne. He tapped her glass with his. "To the sixth race," he toasted, his face still flushed from his own success. He glanced around at the crowd. "Too bad Sylvie has to miss this."

Lise took a small sip. "Where is she?"

"In Madang. I flew her there this morning."

"You're a pilot, too?"

"After McDowell, the best in New Guinea."

"Will Sylvie be back in time for the dance?" Perhaps Sylvie could tell her more about Simon, could somehow explain the pain in his eyes when he spoke of his ex-wife.

Jim shook his head. "Probably not.

"Did you see that heat?" Simon demanded, his gravelly voice accosting her from behind. Lise whirled to face him. Simon's eyes were alight with pleasure.

~*~

"My Uncle Simon's going to win for sure," Connor bubbled, bouncing beside Lise like a puppy on a pogo stick.

If only he would! Then she wouldn't have to fulfil her part in his ridiculous bet. She would do something else for Michael's school to make up for it. Donate some medical supplies, update their equipment, train one of the brothers in rudimentary first aid, anything rather than actually work with the patients.

A lump formed in her throat. Until her father's accident, she had loved spending time with the patients more than anything else. She shuddered and stared at the track. Thinking about the past didn't help.

Would this last race never begin? It seemed an eternity since they had called the winners of the six heats to the starting post. Simon had to win.

There, the official's hand was up.

The starting gun was poised.

Simon's huge stallion snorted and pricked his ears forward. He appeared to have no use for the wild antics of the other horses around him. He was like his owner: cool, serious and alert.

The gun rang out. They were off.

How could they even know where they were going in that cloud of billowing dust? With great effort, Lise could just make out Simon's white shirt amongst the brilliant colors of the other riders.

Crouched low over his mount's neck, Simon seemed to be holding on by the strength of his muscular legs alone. He had drawn the middle track, the worst starting position of all. Jim was to his right and, although her view of Michael was partially blocked, she caught glimpses of his blue shirt next to the inside rail.

Poor Michael. His mare was dancing and lunging and generally behaving very badly. Simon and Jim pressed their heels hard into their horses' sides and applied their riding crops lightly to their mounts' withers, urging their animals away from the pack, away from Michael.

Lise sucked in a ragged breath. They were going too fast, yet neck and neck, they prodded their horses even faster.

A tornado of dust whirled up from beneath the horses' feet and the cheers and encouragement of the crowd threatened to drown out the thunder of their hooves. Flecks of white sweat flew off in the horses' wake as they swept past the spectators on their first lap. Dark patches of damp glistened beneath and around the saddles.

Suddenly, Lise's breath snagged in her throat. Simon's horse had faltered. She was aware of the other horses still speeding around the track, but it suddenly felt as though the race were being run in slow motion.

Simon was off balance, leaning too far forward to stay in the saddle. Lise's fingernails bit into her palms, until, inch by excruciating inch, Simon righted himself.

She couldn't stand any more of this. She couldn't stand here and wait for Simon to be injured. But she couldn't turn away, either. Not until it was over. Not until she knew he was safe.

Simon and his mount took the corner at break-neck speed. Surely he was cutting it too close for safety? Some five feet behind him, a horse stumbled, its rider sliding off and rolling to the side of the track. He lay there motionless for a second or two, then shakily rose to his feet.

The spectators roared.

Lise felt she might faint.

Desperately, she focused her eyes on Simon's white shirt. He bent lower than before over his horse's neck, pressing his heels harder into his horse's sides. Surely, he couldn't go faster, couldn't do this to her.

A ringing began in her ears. He wasn't doing it to her at all. He didn't care what she thought. Her fingers curled into fists. Curled so hard they hurt. The pain was welcome. If her palms hurt, maybe the riders would be spared. Maybe Simon would make it around safely.

Simon and Jim were well out in front now, with Michael making a hopeless attempt to overtake from behind. Then, all at once, Jim's gelding stumbled and the bulk of its body was thrown to the left. Right into the hind quarters of Simon's stallion. Lise clutched Connor's shoulder, her stomach clenching. Both horses hovered on the verge of tumbling over, then Jim's gelding righted itself and veered off the track.

Simon's horse went down, its legs flailing the air.

For what seemed an eternity, Lise could see nothing but a jumble of limbs and hooves as the rest of the field thundered over the downed horse.

There was no sign of Simon.

Lise began to run before her brain had time to command her legs. She ran as though her very life depended on it. Her breath rasped her ears. Dimly, she was aware of other people behind her, calling out for stretchers and medical help. They were slow, far too slow.

A cramp tugged her side. She ignored it. Through the combination of sweat and tears blinding her eyes, the way ahead was a blur. She swept the moisture away with the back of her hand. Stumbling once, she managed, with a fierce effort of will, to keep her balance.

At last she could see him. Not under his horse as she expected, but on the ground motionless, his face too white against the black of his hair. His horse had heaved itself to its feet and stood with its head down, nuzzling Simon's shoulder. It whinnied softly and whirled away as she approached.

She fell on her knees at Simon's side, longing to take him in her arms and kiss the pain away. But she was a doctor.

Swiftly, she took his hand in hers. His pulse was even. He was breathing. His eyes were closed, his lids nearly transparent. His face was too pale, but there was no sign of blood or abrasions. Carefully, she examined his arms, then his legs, moving down the outside and up the inside.

Nothing seemed amiss. She undid a few buttons at the neck and bottom of his shirt, then pulled the shirt free from his pants. Slipping her hand up under the cloth, she felt for injuries: broken ribs, contusions.

She found nothing but skin, warm, firm skin, satin soft to the touch and covered with silky hair. She swallowed hard, her mouth suddenly dry.

"Feels nice."

She gasped.

"But hardly the place," Simon complained. "We should continue this somewhere more comfortable."

She snatched her hand from his skin, her gaze darting to his face.

He lay with his eyes half-open and a slow smile on his lips. No pain clouded his eyes. Instead, they glowed with sultry warmth.

"Don't stop," he instructed lazily. "There's nothing wrong with your bedside manner."

She leaned hard on his chest.

"How dare you!" she whispered fiercely. "You pretended to be hurt!"

"I wasn't pretending." He looked aggrieved. "I think you've bruised my ribs."

She sucked in her breath. "You're lucky that's all."

The others were approaching now, pounding along the track, arms filled with blankets and bearing a stretcher.

"You really do care," he purred. He glanced past her. "I'm all right, mates," he called out, motioning them away with his hand.

Connor raced toward them, and dropped to his knees beside his uncle. His small face was white beneath his freckles.

Simon's expression softened. "I'm fine, Connor. Just a little winded, that's all." He sat up. "Go along to the refreshment tent, will you, and get me a glass of water."

The boy looked dubious.

"And buy an ice cream for yourself. Don't worry, you can leave me here with the good doctor." He smiled directly into Lise's eyes. "She'll take care of me."

Connor did as he was told, glancing back once or twice before sprinting toward the refreshment tent. The men left also, shaking their heads as they retreated the way they had come. Lise knelt in the dirt, frozen to the spot.

"What's the matter?" Simon asked. His warm hand covered hers. "I meant it when I said I'm all right now."

Lise's chest felt strange, as though it might explode if she breathed. Simon ran his hand up her arm to her shoulder.

"What is it?" he demanded softly.

She shook her head, unable to speak.

His fingers tightened on her shoulder. "It's time you told me."

His eyes compelled her, yet their power was frightening. God knew what they'd make her tell him. She struggled to shift her gaze from his, but was unable.

"Tell me," he insisted, unrelentingly gripping her shoulders with both hands. "You must."

He touched her cheek, his caress feather soft. His eyes held the luster of a tropical night and were somehow just as comforting.

"Tell me," he commanded again gently. "Tell me about when your father died."

She stared at him, appalled. How could he know?

He continued to stroke her cheek.

"He fell," she began, his gentleness finally breaking her resolve. She shut her eyes. "From a horse."

"Go on."

Could she say the words? She had kept them within so long, her voice might crack if she tried. "I was home for a holiday after my final term of residency," she managed, trying to fill her dry mouth with moisture. "Dad was breaking in a young stallion." Now the words wouldn't stop. She gulped hugely. "He always liked to do that himself, said the hands wouldn't do it properly. You can ruin a good horse if you don't do it properly."

She opened her eyes. "That's what he said, but that wasn't why he did it. He did it because he wanted to. He always did what he wanted." Her throat prickled with rage. "No matter what my mother said."

"He was like you," she added, furiously aware of Simon's too strong chin, his resolute eyes, his determined body. "He couldn't resist the challenge of taking a chance. It's what he lived for."

"Not quite like me," Simon contradicted quietly.

"Well, this time he lost." She didn't want to hear how her father and Simon were different. "The horse was wild. I begged him to wait until one of the hands got back, but he wouldn't listen to me. And Dad . . . well, he wasn't so young anymore."

"What happened?"

"The horse reared up." She had been over it in her mind a thousand times but the picture never changed. "Dad fell off. I ran to him, expecting him to get up. He always had before." No amount of blinking could stop the tears from filling her eyes. "This time," her voice wobbled, "he didn't. He lay there, blood all around." She would never be able to forget all that blood. "He had hit his head. I tried everything I could think of to stop the bleeding, to get him to come around, but nothing worked. He . . . he died.

"All those years of medical training," she cried out, her throat closing over as she stared helplessly at Simon, "and I couldn't save him." She turned away. She couldn't bear to look at Simon now she'd told him, couldn't bear to see the contempt in his eyes.

He pulled her around to face him. "Do you mean to tell me you've been blaming yourself for your father's death?" His gaze raked hers. "Maybe you should quit if you don't have better sense than that."

She stiffened.

"Did you speak to anyone about this?" he demanded. "Someone who could help you get it in perspective?"

She shook her head.

He glared at her. "Do you honestly believe you could have saved him?"

She searched her heart for the answer to his

question, desperate to find one that made sense. "I don't know," she said numbly.

Simon put his arms around her. "Let him go, Lise," he said, his voice softening to a whisper. "There was nothing you could have done, no matter how much you loved him."

She didn't want to hear his words. She didn't want him to hold her so tightly. Tears burned her cheeks. Her fists pounded against his chest.

He simply held her closer.

Again and again she pummeled him, stopping only when her strength was gone. Her chest heaving, she could no longer struggle against his warmth. But she couldn't stop sobbing. His shirt was wet with her pain. His hand caressed her back, soothing her, comforting her until his arms no longer felt like chains that bound, but a safety net to catch her.

She clutched his shirt. She had never let herself confide like this before. Not with anyone. Before this moment, there'd never been anyone she could tell.

She swept the tears from her eyes, and with a final hiccup, managed to stop crying at last. She pushed his arms from around her and she grew chilled, as though clouds had moved in to cover up the sky. She glanced upward. The sun beat down as fiercely as before.

She was afraid to meet his eyes. If she saw contempt in them, or worse yet, pity, she would leave on the next plane. Her heart thudding as though she had just completed a marathon, she forced herself to look.

"Feeling better?" he asked gently.

She nodded, amazed to find she did.

For an instant, relief showed in his eyes, mixing with the sympathy. Then just as swiftly, his expression turned to triumph.

"In that case," Simon said. "We'll have a lot to talk about tonight at the dance."

She stared at him, baffled. There was nothing more to talk about.

"You see, Dr. Dawson," he whispered, leaning so close she could see her reflection in the inky blackness of his pupils, "Michael has won."

Chapter Eight

Simon was early. Lise drummed her fingertips against the window sill nervously, shy about facing him. She twitched back the curtain a little more and peeked out at him from the oblong window at the top of the landing.

Simon and her aunt stood talking at the edge of the Sisters' experimental coffee plot, just visible in the moonlight. From the animated expression on her aunt's face, they could only be discussing the new strains of coffee the vocational students had planted.

Simon was elegant in his light trousers and loose-fitting linen jacket, but when he threw back his head and laughed at something Aunt Cecile said, Lise's breath caught in her throat. From this distance, she couldn't see what she normally saw, the determination etched in every line of his face. The night's shadows made him seem younger somehow, more carefree.

Simon bent and stroked the head of the large male setter at his feet. It wagged its tail furiously, sidling sideways into Simon's legs, then sat on his foot. Strangely, none of the dogs had barked when Simon drove in.

Lise headed for the stairs. Halfway down she paused, grimacing at her reflection in the glass of a framed picture of Saint Mark. She tugged at her curls.

If she could even occasionally cajole them into some semblance of order, she'd be satisfied, but tonight was obviously not the night. She opened the front door, blinking as she stepped into the pool of brightness cast from the porch light above her head.

Simon saw her and moved toward her after murmuring a few words to Aunt Cecile. He took the stairs two at a time to stand beside her on the porch.

His presence electrified her senses; the sight of him, and when his hand took hold of hers, his touch.

"Good evening, Lise," he said, his normally gravelly voice as smooth as velvet. "Ready to go?"

"Yes," she replied, suddenly excited, her spirits inexplicably rising. She would forget her worries and concentrate on having a good time, if only for this evening.

She placed her hand in Simon's and accompanied him down the stairs to where her aunt waited.

"You look lovely, dear," Cecile murmured, her eyes crinkling when she smiled. She gave Lise a swift hug.

"Drive safely," her aunt admonished, as Simon opened the car door for Lise. "The roads are so dangerous at night."

They didn't feel dangerous. Not tonight. Not sitting next to Simon. For once, he drove slowly. Wrapped in a cocoon of security, she felt safer in this car, with this man, than she had ever felt before.

~*~

The twin flames of the candles glinted dangerously in Simon's eyes. Together with the scar down his cheek, he appeared wicked, excitingly, forbiddenly wicked.

"You could be a gypsy," Simon announced, leaning back in his chair.

"I beg your pardon?"

"With your hair!" He reached forward again and twined one curl around his finger. "In this candlelight. It's not hard to imagine you pirouetting around a campfire enticing young men to dance."

Lise held her head still. The touch of his hand on her hair left her breathless.

"And your eyes!" Slightly rough against her

smoothness, his fingers slid across her temple until they reached her forehead. He brushed her curls back, then let his hand drop to the nape of her neck. "So dark and all-knowing. What do you see, Dr. Dawson, that the rest of us don't?"

"You might not want to know, Mr. McDowell." There was heat where his skin rested against hers. It was all she could do to keep her voice from trembling. "It might not be flattering." She didn't dare tell him what she saw when she looked at him. She was starting to see far too much she liked.

He laughed, then inspected her eyes. "Shall I tell you what I see? I see a wild side struggling to escape." His expression grew serious. "Just think how exhilarating it would be to break free."

She wanted no part of any wild side. It was dangerous. She had seen what it did to her father.

"If I were a fortune teller," Simon continued, "I'd say you have many hidden depths."

"Everyone has hidden depths, Simon." He certainly did. "I do know I can get passionately angry, but so can you. It doesn't take a fortune teller to know that."

He leaned even closer. So close Lise could see just when his eyes darkened to ebony.

"It's not anger I'm interested in arousing."

The sounds from the room faded. For the space of a heartbeat, she longed to let herself take the chance. But this was Simon, a man who took more risks than even her father, a man who broke hearts and remained free. She stared into his eyes as deeply as she dared. He was a man who had seen pain and wasn't about to risk that again any more than she. Swallowing hard, she jerked her gaze away.

"Care to dance, Lise?" Jim materialized from the crowd swirling beyond their table, his voice breaking the suddenly strained silence. Lise muffled a deep sigh of relief. She couldn't respond to what Simon had said. She didn't dare. He had the ability to make her feel again, and that in itself was dangerous.

"You don't mind, do you, McDowell?" Jim asked, glumly acknowledging Simon. His gaze shifted back to Lise. "You can't monopolize the prettiest woman here."

Simon drew his hand back from Lise's face and shrugged. "It's entirely up to Lise."

She stood so abruptly her chair almost tipped backward. She had to dance. If she stayed with Simon any longer, his spell would engulf her. Already, it was all but impossible to leave. Clutching Jim's hand for direction, she backed away.

The music had begun by the time they reached the dance floor. The small building throbbed with sound. Voices rang out as people commented on this year's winner and argued as to who had the best chance next year. Glasses tinkled from the tables surrounding the parquet floor. Toasts were proposed for everything and nothing. Laughter spiraled through the room.

But Lise didn't laugh.

She sucked in her lower lip and tried to shift her concentration onto Jim. She tried to follow his rhythm, but it was as if she were out of sync. Her head began to pound. Shadows formed and reformed as the dancers spun, frenzied planes and lines crossing and crisscrossing her face as the light from countless flickering candles was blocked then set free.

She tried to focus on the movement of her feet, on the feel of Jim's hand on her waist. Anything! But all she was really aware of were Simon's dark eyes watching her. Eyes looking at her, through her. Dancers moved in front of her, blocking him from her.

She strained to see around Jim and caught a glimpse of Simon's dark head. He sat alone. Unmoving. Untouchable. Longing flooded through her. The need to study the contours of

Simon's face with her own hands and feel the smooth-rough texture of his skin was overwhelming. She wrenched her gaze away, her breathing ragged.

The rhythm of the music was elusive, yet it seemed to Lise as though she had been dancing for an eternity. Her skin was a sheen of perspiration and her black sheath clung to her body. She swept her hair from her forehead, but it bounced back, as always, reacting to moisture with defiance.

Jim held her waist loosely at first, then his hand drifted lower. She frowned and pulled away. His grip tightened, then, with a crash of cymbals, the music ended.

She wiggled free.

"Another dance?" he suggested, reaching for her, claiming her. She stepped backward, eluding him. "No thanks," she panted. "It's far too hot to dance anymore."

"Want to slip outside for some cool air?"

"No," she stated. "I should go back to my table. Simon will be—"

"Simon hasn't missed you."

She glanced at her table and found he was right.

Sylvie stood next to Simon's chair, a skin-tight red dress revealing every curve as she leaned toward him. Her scarlet-tipped fingernails drummed a tune on his arm. Shocking jealousy raged through Lise, cooling her hot skin and leaving her clammily cold.

"I thought Sylvie was on the coast," she said stiffly. She didn't, couldn't care this intensely.

"She finished early," Jim said.

Simon glanced up then, his dark gaze locking with Lise's. He motioned toward their table as though informing her the dance was over.

Lise met the anger crackling through her with relief. She turned back to Jim. "I will dance, after all."

With a satisfied smile, he put his arms around her in a way Lise didn't like. She didn't like, either, the way his fingers traced slow circles along her spine. The music was wrong, too. It was off-key, neither fast nor slow, neither one thing nor the other. Impossible to dance to. Because Jim wasn't Simon, Lise realized miserably.

She stepped backward and away, bumping into another couple. A strong hand grabbed her wrist and whirled her from Jim's arms.

Simon.

He pulled her firmly toward him.

"It's my dance, Mathews," he growled.

"How dare you?" Lise's protest came out

breathless, as though some part of her delighted in his arrogance.

"What do you get if you don't dare?" Simon challenged, gathering her into his arms. "Nothing, that's what." He whispered these last words as though she were not the only person he had to convince, as though a battle raged within him as well.

Dare. The word echoed in her head as he twirled her away. Dare . . . dare . . . dare . . .

Then the music changed and a wild, syncopated beat pulsated through the building, crashing around Lise and over her, under her, too, lifting her against her will and forcing her to participate in the reckless mood of the dance.

Simon moved with a grace and strength that set him apart. He had only to touch her, on her back or on her waist, for her to flow in the direction he sent her.

She had never danced like this before. Her anger, her uncertainty, her longing, fueled an energy she hadn't known she possessed. His touch ignited a fire only possible to assuage by movement. His eyes urged her to be wild, to give herself to her passion.

She twisted, she turned, she dipped, she stood tall, her awareness of her body filling her with pride. It was intoxicating knowing Simon watched as her hips undulated in front of him, seeing desire burn in his eyes as his gaze swept upward over her stomach toward her breasts. Her nipples pushed taut against the fabric of her dress, flaunting and enticing in a manner completely foreign to her. It was as if no one else existed but the two of them.

Simon slid his jacket off and flung it over a chair beside the dance floor. He loosened his tie and undid the top button on his shirt, his other hand still holding her waist firmly.

The dark hair on his chest sprang up, freed from the constraints of civilized attire. His pulse pounded in the hollow of his neck, and his hips moved with the primitive fluidity of the jungle. They took away not only her breath, but also her will to be cautious.

Dancing with him, she felt capable of anything. Then the music died.

Lise stood motionless, locked in the circle of Simon's embrace. Her breath echoed his. Her heart throbbed in an identical rhythm.

It took her a moment to realize the beat pulsing through her body was not her heart but the beginning of a new song. Simon pulled her toward him, slowly, deliberately, sensuously. One hand engulfed her fingers while the other rested on the small of her back.

Magnetic energy filled the space between them, drawing her into it, drawing her into him. She held herself ramrod straight and resisted the pull, for if she surrendered, she'd be lost.

But he allowed no resistance. He dipped her backward so that she leaned into and away from him, trusting him to keep her from falling.

Trusting him.

She stared up into his eyes. How could she trust?

He raised her up again, their bodies close, her breasts flat against his chest and her eyes level with his chin. Her heart ceased its beat, held motionless with the cessation of real time.

Her cheek touched his chest. His breath warmed the hollow below her ear and stirred sweet sensations throughout her body. She trembled at the taut strength of him. The hairs on her arms stood upright as they brushed against the soft material of his clothing. He released her hand and encircled her body with both arms, both hands now resting lightly on the base of her spine.

Her hands, thus freed, found their way up his chest to his shoulders, then to the edge of his shirt collar. His silky hair tickled and tantalized her fingers, but she kept them motionless, curling them against the back of his neck.

The thread of a single saxophone wove through the intricate music, solitary and forlorn. Lise shuddered, clinging closer to Simon, seeking his warmth.

The sax hung on the peak of its highest note until she could bear no more of its anguish. Then the music spiraled downward, gathering speed and warmth as it descended. Simon stared down at her, his tight lips reflecting the agony of the song, his eyes black with pain.

She closed her eyes to shut out that pain and he relaxed against her, as though everything he would rather not see was gone. His heart thumped against her ear, and gradually, smoothly, his fingers fanned out over her buttocks. He groaned, pressing her hips against his own until they moved as one.

A sigh as soft as a whisper escaped her lips. Against her will, her body pressed closer yet, Simon's nearness awakening a fire within.

She burned.

Then without warning, the song ended. She clung to Simon, sensing in him the same reluctance to part. Other couples moved off the floor, but she and Simon stood motionless, caught in each other's arms.

With an uncertain heart, Lise pulled away.

Simon raised his fingers to her jaw and traced

a line down her taut throat to the neckline of her dress.

"Let's go outside," he suggested hoarsely.

Instead of slowing, her heart beat faster. He took her hand in his and wove through the crowd, holding her close against his side as they swept through the glass doors to the patio. Her body betrayed her, coming alive where it touched his.

It should have been dark outside, but millions of stars turned it into a fairyland. Magical. But magic never lasted. With a rush of unease, Lise glanced at Simon's profile.

He plucked a single scarlet blossom from the hibiscus hedge and tucked it tenderly into her hair.

"I was right," he said, his voice filled with wonder. "You are a gypsy." His lips brushed her forehead. "You've bewitched me."

"Don't!" Her voice shook.

He frowned. "Why not?"

It seemed impossible to look into his eyes and say what needed to be said. "That dance was a mistake," she managed.

"Why?" he demanded again, his voice harsh against the velvet night air.

"We'd better go in," she said, not wanting to answer. She turned from him, escaping.

"Not yet." He reached for her. "The moon's out. It'd be a shame to waste it."

It was impossible to think when he looked at her like that: his face taut with desire, his eyes luminous, his lips full . . . descending . . . For one endless moment, Lise thought she could resist, but that thought died when his lips touched hers. They were hard, searching lips. Insistent lips. They played her mouth like a tune, demanding just the right song in return.

But that song would destroy her. She wrenched away. "I want to go in," she insisted.

Simon put his hand on Lise's waist, stopping her. She was breathing hard, as though she were afraid. He could understand her fear. He felt it too. But he couldn't stop himself from reaching past it, toward her, for her. She was like the color red to a bull. He knew she was danger, but he charged anyway.

"Running away gets you nowhere," he whispered. No matter how much he had tried to run, tried to forget, the memories still remained. His lips tightened and he stood his ground. "Besides, I have something for you."

Her gaze locked with his, but her body was poised, ready to bolt if he released her gaze. He drew the drawstring bag from his pocket and tipped the contents into his hand. Her gaze dropped. He looked down then, too.

Her opal lay translucent against his skin, streaks of pink and blue winking in the moonlight. She stared at it for a moment, not saying a word, then met his gaze once more.

"My opal," she breathed.

"Fire embedded in ice," he said hoarsely. "Like you."

Something like pain flickered across her face.

"I added the chain. One that won't break this time." It had been his mother's. Had become his when she died. It seemed somehow right to give it to Lise.

Again the pain showed itself, hit her eyes first and stayed there. She made no move to take the opal.

"It's just a necklace, Lise," he growled, moving behind her. Her curls felt like silk as he lifted her hair. His fingers burned where they brushed against her skin. He draped the necklace around her neck and locked the clasp, the stone settling in the valley between her breasts.

She twisted away and faced him. Wordlessly, she shook her head.

"It won't hurt you," he insisted.

"It could have hurt you, getting it back."

"You can't be afraid." If he said it often enough, perhaps he'd believe it, too. Perhaps then he could convince himself that what had happened with Marion wouldn't happen again. "You have to grab hold of life or it'll leave you behind." He wanted to touch Lise, to hold her, to feel her life force. Anything to silence the voice cautioning him to beware.

He reached out his hand and touched her arm. Fear shafted through him, mixed with desire. Straightening his shoulders, he willed it to pass.

As though his touch prompted her, she reached for her opal. It seemed to throb beneath her fingertips like blood through a vein. It seemed to give her courage.

"Is that what you did?" she demanded, her mouth twisting.

"What do you mean?"

"Did you grab hold of life, your kind of life?" Her expression grew haunted as though the very idea terrified her. "Is that what happened with your wife?"

"What do you know of my wife?"

"Only that you were married."

Married was something different than what he and Marion had shared. Married was something wonderful.

"Is that why your wife left?"

He drew back, his body stiffening. "I won't

discuss my wife with you."

"Too painful?" she taunted, her eyes condemning him.

"None of your business."

She looked as feverish as he felt. Her face was white and a sheen of perspiration covered her skin. The hand clutching the opal shook, but she lifted her chin. "You brought her back from Sydney after Connor's parents died?" She'd phrased it like a question, but she seemed to know.

Well, she didn't know.

"Didn't she want to come?"

Laughter escaped his lips, but he couldn't conceal the bitterness touching its edges. "She wanted to come all right."

A line formed on Lise's brow. "To take care of the baby—Connor?"

"No," he said numbly. "She didn't come for Connor."

Lise frowned.

"She was a doctor," he growled. "A doctor like you. One who didn't heal, who did research instead."

It was as though he had slapped Lise. On her face, white patches formed on red, and with a low cry, she twirled and disappeared through the glass doors, vanishing into the crush of dancers beyond.

Chapter Nine

Blemish medication! At first glance, there seemed little else in the first aid station. Lise stared glumly at the tubes of cream in her hand, then back at the huge crate blocking the entrance to the pharmaceutical supply room. The return address of a Chicago hospital was printed clearly on the crate in black felt pen.

Disgusted, Lise tipped the tubes back into the crate.

"Don't worry."

At the sound of Simon's voice, her heart clenched. She raised her head. He was leaning against the door jamb as though last night had never happened.

Her fingers sought her opal, her heart glad it was back where it belonged. If she hung onto it tightly, perhaps she would find the strength she needed.

"They don't have even one pimple between the lot of them!" she exclaimed.

Simon smiled, and the warmth in his smile heated the room. "The students will love this stuff," he said, stepping forward and crouching down beside her.

So close. Too close. The morning scent of him, his soap, his aftershave, floated around her. She leaned away, longing to lean closer.

He reached in front of her and picked up a tube. Unscrewing the cap, he squeezed a small portion onto his hand, then swiped an ivory streak across his tanned cheek. "It makes the best damn face paint they'll ever see," he said, his smile growing to a grin.

"Face paint!" Her own lips trembled in the beginnings of a smile, then his arm brushed hers and the smile died.

"Bilas, decoration. The boys will arrive with every ache and pain they can think up in order to get a tube of this stuff as a reward." His face lost its teasing look, grew serious. "You'll catch the tropical ulcers sooner, before they infect so badly antibiotics are needed."

Her attention was caught.

"Besides," he said, his eyes glinting with satisfaction. "We received a letter full of apologies that the wrong crate had been shipped. Another one, full of penicillin this time, is on its way." He held up the tube. "But in the meantime, no sense wasting this."

Nothing was wasted here. She liked that. It didn't seem to matter that the people didn't have much. The one thing they did have was the ability to achieve happiness. They made it look so simple.

"This crate needs shifting," Simon said. "I'll do it before I go."

"Thanks," Lise muttered, biting off the protest springing to her lips. To get into that supply room, she needed his help.

"You'll have to move."

She shifted so that he could squeeze past her into the narrow space between the box and the cupboard. He edged the crate out a few inches to give himself more room, then bent his knees, put his arms around and under the crate, and heaved.

It was as awkward as it was heavy. Simon's shoulders strained, and below his khaki shorts, his brown legs corded with exertion.

"Let me help," Lise offered, grabbing hold of one end of the box. It was only her fingers that touched his, but the shock went through her entire body.

"Leave it," he growled.

She backed hastily away, pressing against the wall as Simon moved past her and dumped the crate on the work bench in the middle of the room.

"Simon, we have to talk."

He turned to face her, his shoulders and back stiff, his eyes narrowing. "I thought we said plenty last night."

"We did," she agreed. "But we didn't say it all."

"All?" His face darkened. "It was enough. I didn't expect to find you here this morning."

"I told you, I always keep my promises."

He swore softly, then thrust out his hands and gripped her shoulder. "Life is more than promises. Promises are useless unless you know what you want!"

"So why am I here?" she demanded.

"I'm not sure." His jaw hardened. "And I don't think you know either. When you do—" He let go of her so suddenly she staggered. "—we'll talk." He pushed past her and out the door, anger following in his wake like a force field.

There was no sound now but the echo of her pounding heart. She hugged her body with her arms, attempting to warm where no warmth remained. For what seemed an eternity, she simply stood, staring at the door through which Simon had disappeared.

Until at last, she glanced around the empty room, struggling to focus on something other than her thoughts, struggling to connect. She walked toward the supply room. It was a place to start, a place to get her bearings. If she could work, then perhaps her thoughts would disappear.

She pushed open the door. Bottled medicines were stacked on shelves overflowing in disarray. Lise ran her finger over the counter top, grimacing when she hit a sticky patch. Before she could even start to bring order to the other room, she had a major cleaning job.

"Hello, Miss Dawson."

She spun around, startled. "Connor." She took a deep breath. "What brings you here? Is something wrong?"

"With me?" the boy demanded indignantly. "I never get sick."

Lise smiled. Connor had obviously forgotten his recent bout with malaria.

"Uncle Simon sent me."

"What do you mean, sent you?" Lise asked, her smile collapsing in on itself.

"He said you might need help." The boy's gaze darted around the room, then returned to meet hers. "He was right!"

The hair on the back of her neck bristled, snagging against her collar as she turned her head.

Connor stared up at her, his face wrinkling

with worry.

Guilt pierced Lise's anger. She hadn't meant to frighten Connor. No matter how she felt about Simon, the boy was just doing what he was told. She mustered a smile.

"Thank you for offering, Connor. I could use your help."

"Great! Uncle Simon told me to stay, no matter what. He said you might want company, but if he came again you'd send him away with a flea in his ear." He peered up at her apprehensively. "You won't put a flea in my ear will you?"

"No," she promised, chuckling. Simon McDowell had a nerve but he couldn't have sent a better ambassador.

"So where do I start? I could bandage something."

Lise suppressed another grin. "No patients here now, Connor. Could you get that bucket from beneath the sink and start scrubbing the counters?"

His face drooped, but he took out the bucket, filled it with soap and water and proceeded to clean as a sailor would swab a deck, with more energy than finesse.

Lise watched him, sucking her bottom lip between her teeth. He had the look of his uncle. The same determined tilt to the jaw, the same intense eyes. She shook her head. Forget the man!

~*~

A soft sound, a hesitant shuffling of feet, was all that warned her before two enormous brown eyes set in a coffee-colored face peeped shyly around the door jamb. Lise held her breath, not daring to even blink, for if she did, the boy might disappear.

"Come in," she said, glad the clinic was ready, grateful for all the help Connor had given her the day before.

The boy sidled around the door, dragging one foot as though poised for flight. His instep was swollen and sore, his mouth tight with pain. She had been dreading her first patient, but how could she fear a child like this?

"Sit here," she said with a smile, and gestured to the bench lining one wall. "Let me have a look."

The boy perched so tentatively on the edge of his seat she was certain he would fall off. He was too young, surely, to be in high school. But of course, there was an elementary school on the mission station, as well as the laborers and their families.

Lise crouched in front of the boy and gently

lifted his inflamed appendage. He flinched, the jagged gash on his foot extending nearly two inches along the soft inner sole.

"How did you do this?" she asked.

"Fishing," the boy whispered, his dark gaze jerking shyly away from hers.

Lise frowned. "Did you catch your foot with your hook?"

"Hook?" The boy's gaze returned to her, startled. "I don't have any hooks."

"How do you catch your fish?" she asked, dabbing antiseptic gently on to the wound as she spoke. If she could keep the child talking, he might not notice when it hurt.

"I sit in the water with my heels together and as the fish come downstream, I wave them toward my body with my hands."

She glanced skeptically at him.

"I caught four today," he said earnestly.

"Four! Where are they?"

"Outside."

She glanced toward the door. The sun no longer poured in. Simon's body was blocking it. He was watching her, his face a mask. She swallowed hard. How long had he been there?

"Do you want to see?" the boy asked, dragging her attention back to him.

"Sure." With suddenly trembling fingers, she

wrapped a snowy bandage around his foot, then stood and moved to the door. Beyond Simon, on a fishing line tied to a branch of a tree, dangled four fish.

"You're still here, then," Simon said.

She forced her gaze to meet his. "Did you think I wouldn't be?"

He shrugged.

She moved back toward the boy, aware of Simon's gaze on her back, aware of a weakness in her knees.

"Your fish are wonderful," she said softly to the child, giving his shoulder a gentle pat. "There. You're all done. If you keep the dressing clean and dry, your cut will be better in no time." If only it were as simple to heal a soul. "Come back tomorrow and I'll have another look."

The boy seemed as reluctant to leave as she was to see him go, for when he was gone, she'd be alone with Simon. Which was more difficult to handle than doctoring. The child remained seated, his head bobbing up and down shyly, before finally, he raised expressive eyes to hers.

"Would you like one of my fish?" he asked.

Moisture pricked her eyes. He had worked so hard for the fish, yet he wanted to give one to her. She blinked, not wanting to raise her hand to her tears, not wanting Simon to see her cry.

"I'd love a fish," she said, keeping her voice even. She turned to the crate on the table and rummaged through its contents. "But only if you accept something from me. How about this?" She held up a tube of the blemish medication, opened it and smeared a streak across the back of her hand.

A grin lit the boy's face. He hobbled past Simon, cut the biggest fish from his line, then limped back in again and laid it on the table. Eagerly, he held out his hand for the tube. When it was in his palm, he stared at it for a long moment, as though unable to believe his good fortune.

"Thank you, brother . . . er, sister, er . . ."

"My name's Dr. Dawson," Lise said, stifling a grin.

The boy bobbed his head in another grin and sketched a swift wave before disappearing through the door. Leaving her alone. With Simon.

"You did well." Simon's voice was warm. His eyes were warm, too.

Heat flamed Lise's face. She turned away. Where had it come from, all that admiration?

"You looked as though you were enjoying yourself."

She sucked in a swift breath, the truth catching her unawares. She faced Simon, found he was closer now. Too close to evade. Too close to deny.

"I did enjoy it," she said, her voice cracking. "But the problem was small. What happens when something big goes wrong? What happens then?"

He looked at her long and hard. "You'll handle it," he said at last, his eyes filled with certainty. "It'll be fine."

~*~

Lise lowered the blinds in a vain attempt to block the heat as sun poured in through the clinic's louvered windows. The crowded waiting room became even more claustrophobic than before, the bench packed with students and village people silently waiting with round dark eyes.

Simon was right. They did desperately need a hospital here. She'd been running the haus sik for only two weeks, but already she had treated over one hundred and fifty patients. Nothing very serious so far, nothing she couldn't handle with the materials she had on hand, nothing that made her blood run cold at the mere thought of making a mistake.

And Simon had been there to help. She glanced across the room to where he dangled a baby from one arm while reaching into a tin of treats with the other. It should have been incongruous, Simon with a small baby, but somehow it wasn't. He was comfortable, practiced.

A young girl waited patiently at his side, her gaze never leaving the lollipop he held out to her. Too young to be the mother of the child. Must be a sister, a cousin even, called in to help while the mother worked in the gardens.

Lise had come to depend on Simon. He slipped in and out of the haus sik like a spirit, never staying long, but somehow always being on hand when she needed him most, when the crowd was the largest, when the bench was overflowing.

Connor came too. The boy moved between his uncle and her like quicksilver, chatting, boiling water, presenting her with bandages. He kept up a steady stream of chatter with the students who came in, breaking the ice, making them feel at home. He was useful.

One more thing Simon had been right about.

Lise pressed her lips tight as she examined the thickly muscled leg of the youth in front of her and felt the hard lump of infection surrounding the open sore of a nasty tropical ulcer. It was caked with pus and needed to be soaked to get the hard core softened.

Simon appeared at her side with a bowl of hot water. She immersed her cloth in it, careful to keep her hand a safe distance from his. When he got too close, her skin seemed to glow as though warming from some inner fire. It was dangerous, that glow.

She wrung out her cloth again and again, but still she was unable to remove the head of the ulcer and wipe clean the crater it would leave behind. This one was down to the bone.

She looked up and met Simon's eyes. The heat started in the pit of her stomach this time, as though two matches had been rubbed together and ignited. She dropped her gaze quickly and asked for a pot of the tar-like substance she used as a poultice to draw the infection from the ulcer.

The smell of the medication was just what she needed to wipe all awareness of heat from her mind. Its scent was so putrid she sucked in the air she needed to breathe through her mouth. Too late, she realized that while the black goop was effective on ulcers, it had no impact at all on the fire within.

*

Lise followed the last patient to the door and turned off the light. She stood for a moment, propped wearily against the door jamb. The sun was already halfway down the sky. She was glad she had sent Connor home. For the two weeks he'd been helping, he had stayed far too long each day. He would stay until dark if she let him.

She waved to some students walking in from the school gardens, dragging their shovels behind them and chatting together in their own dialects. On the driveway behind them a cloud of dust spiraled up.

A vehicle.

Lise straightened and peered into the lowering sun. Only one person she knew drove that fast.

"Evening, Lise," Simon said, his Jeep rumbling to a halt in front of the clinic.

"Evening," she replied, smiling at him.

He swung down from the front seat and approached her. He seemed taller, broader, and strangely stern. Lise's legs seemed to lose their ability to keep her upright. Stupid to let him affect her like this, stupid to have no control. She braced herself against the doorway as she would in an earthquake.

"How did everything go today?"

"Fine. Why do you ask?"

He took another step closer.

She raised her eyebrows, willing him to stay where he was, willing her heart to cease its frantic pounding.

"Have you changed your mind yet about staying on and working in the new hospital?" he asked, answering her question with his own.

Her heart ceased its beat. "No."

"You seem to like the people."

"I made a promise, that's all."

He flinched.

She fought an inclination to smooth the tension from his face. "I'm doing a good job, Simon."

"I know you're doing a good job." He seemed to grow taller, his body straightening so stiffly she was afraid it might snap. "I just don't want to be caught unawares when it ends." His expression told her he expected the ax to descend this minute, that he'd welcome a finish to the suspense.

Lise straightened, too, relieved she didn't fall, grateful for the pride infusing her legs with strength. "I've not completed our bargain yet."

His face darkened. "If you're doing this simply out of duty, you might as well quit now. I won't hold you to your promise." A nerve below his temple jerked, as though he expected a response he couldn't bear to hear.

"You're a fine one to talk of duty!"

"What do you mean?"

"Why are you in New Guinea?" she demanded.

"To take care of Connor, of course."

"And duty has nothing to do with that?"

"Of course not," he said. "You know how I feel about Connor."

She did know how he felt about the boy. It was obvious in every line of his face, every nuance of expression, every soft word and swift caress.

"But why New Guinea?" she asked. How he felt about Connor was irrelevant to where they lived. "Why not somewhere else?" With someone else. His wife.

He gripped her arm, his anger searing through to her skin. "Living in New Guinea is part of Connor's heritage, part of what he had with his parents. I don't want him to lose that connection."

The boys returning from the school gardens were beginning to stare. They walked past in small groups, watching, whispering.

Lise jerked her arm from Simon's grip. "We'd better go inside. We have an audience out here."

Simon turned and glowered at the boys.

Lowering their heads, they moved swiftly toward their dormitory. Lise stepped into the clinic and Simon followed, shutting the door behind him.

She faced him, stunned that the moment had come so unexpectedly, terrified to ask the question, but needing to know the answer.

"And your wife?" Her question emerged in a whisper.

"Ex-wife," he growled, his eyes hardening. "What about her?"

"Where is she now?"

"Australia," he spat out, making it sound like Siberia.

"Why did she leave?" Lise held her breath, not sure he would tell her, not sure she really wanted to know.

The color ebbed from Simon's face. "She had finished what she came for."

"If you loved her, why didn't you go with her?"

His face went blank, as though he had retreated behind some invisible wall.

"People don't always love the same," he finally answered, his voice tight. "Don't want the same."

Icy cold crept through Lise's heart. "Perhaps you didn't love her enough."

He looked at her strangely, then his face shuttered. "Perhaps you're right. Perhaps I didn't give her what she needed."

The phone rang.

Lise crossed in front of Simon and picked up the heavy black receiver. "Hello?"

Chapter Ten

"It's for you," Lise said, holding out the receiver to Simon. "Connor. He sounds upset."

Simon was at her side in a single stride. He took the receiver from her hand and listened without interruption.

With growing unease, Lise watched the frown lines deepen on Simon's forehead. What if Connor was . . . No, if he was hurt, he wouldn't be on the phone. But what then?

"Where?" Simon demanded brusquely. "Is John with her?"

Simon was so alert, so tense, so worried. Grimmer, in fact, than she had ever seen him before. He suddenly threw the receiver back into its cradle, turned, and headed for the door.

"Get your bag," he said tersely.

Lise's heart fluttered. An emergency. With no one to take care of it but herself.

"Simon," she said, hating the sound of strain in her own voice. "Connor's all right, isn't he?" If anything happened to the boy . . .

"Connor's fine! Hurry. You have a baby to deliver."

His voice was strained, also. He spat out the words, as though that were the only possible way he could get them out.

The heat drained from Lise's face. She threw the things she needed into her black bag, then raced after Simon, her stomach leaden. She slammed the clinic door behind her and locked it. Simon was already behind the wheel of his Jeep, the engine roaring. A new group of students had stopped to watch.

She couldn't seem to open the Jeep's door. Her fingers numb, she fumbled with the handle. Simon shoved it open from the inside.

"Come on," he said, glancing at her sharply. "You're not going to freeze on me, are you?"

She climbed into her seat, her breathing fast and shallow.

"This isn't the time to indulge yourself."

Anger swept over Lise in a single wave, pushing anxiety in front of it like so much rubbish. Taking a deep breath, she held on to it, determined not to let him see how terrified she was. If she could hide her fear from her colleagues and instructors in those last few weeks of her residency, she could hide it from him.

"Well?" he demanded.

"You're wasting time," she said, staring straight ahead so he wouldn't see her eyes.

"Good girl." He shifted the Jeep into gear and stepped on the gas.

"Where are we going?" she asked, playing with the latch on her bag, ignoring the warmth sweeping through her at his words.

"My place."

"Your place?" She shot him a quick look.

"It's Rose, my bossboy John's wife. She's in labor." A line appeared between his eyebrows. "A lot of pain."

Lise's muscles stiffened with dread. Children were born all the time, but the list of things that could go wrong was endless. What if she had to do a Caesarian? What if Rose hemorrhaged? What if she froze as she had with her father?

"Is she still at home?"

"No," he said, the line between his brows deepening. "She's in the coffee fields."

Lise slumped against her seat. She'd forgotten, for a moment, where she was.

"Where did you expect her to be? In a hospital?"

There was no hospital.

"In the coffee fields," she repeated, her voice high. She stared at him. "You have her working?"

His lips tightened. "She chose to continue on. Most women here do. They're incredible."

The respect in his voice was strong. "They work right up to the end and as often as not give birth in the fields. But she's not due for another six weeks."

"Go faster." Had those words come from her mouth?

Simon pressed his foot harder on the accelerator. He looked as black as the devil, only this time she could see what he truly was: a white knight.

Simon took the turn into his drive at breakneck speed. When the car plunged through a deep pothole Lise's head hit the ceiling.

"How far now?" she asked, speaking through clenched teeth so as not to bite off her tongue.

"She's in the south field close to the river."

Lise clutched her bag, sucking in her belly in an effort to quell her queasiness. Perhaps visualizing the scene, focusing on a happy conclusion, would make everything go as it should.

She had done her stint in maternity during training and had loved it. It was usually such a happy wing in a hospital. And when things went wrong, there were specialists to help out.

But here, her gaze swept over the endless rows of coffee bushes, there were no specialists.

Workers lined the dirt track, making their way back to their huts for their evening meal.

She didn't recognize John at first, didn't notice the short, stubble-faced figure waving to catch their attention, not until Simon stopped. Her brain felt fuzzy, caught in the maze of the past.

John hurried around the vehicle to Simon's open window and began speaking so swiftly in pidgin English, Lise understood nothing. Simon stepped out of the Jeep and placed his hand on his bossboy's shoulder. His touch seemed to calm the worried man. John began to speak more coherently and after listening intently, Simon motioned to his bossboy to lead the way. The frantic man started forward, glancing back at Simon continuously as though to reassure himself his employer was there.

Lise scrambled out of the Jeep and Simon took her bag in one hand and her arm with the other. She was grateful for his touch. Together with his warmth, it gave her strength. And she needed strength for she hadn't ceased trembling since Connor had called. She ducked beneath the branch Simon had plucked aside and followed after him along a snakelike path.

They found Rose lying huddled in a small clearing between two rows of coffee bushes. The branches of two shade trees met some seven feet above her head, giving her shelter a natural roof. The last rays of the afternoon sun filtered between the branches, touching the pregnant woman with their warmth.

But when Rose lifted her head and faced them, Lise blanched. However tranquil the spot, its peace hadn't permeated the laboring woman. Rose's eyes were filled with fear, naked and intense.

Lise dropped to her knees at Rose's side and picked up her hand. It was cold and clammy, yet the young woman's skin was covered in a sheen of perspiration. The rich hues of her black skin had lightened to a chalky grey and her face was pinched and tight.

Lise stroked Rose's arm, murmuring to her in a low voice. The laboring woman didn't understand her words, but she spoke them anyway, praying her reassurances would come true.

Then she turned to Simon and her body chilled. He hadn't moved from the edge of the clearing. His shoulders were so stiff he could have been a statue. His face was tense and set, his eyes black with pain.

This wasn't the Simon she knew; the Simon she needed.

"What is it?" she asked, dread clogging her throat.

He shook his head, his eyelids shuttering all expression.

Rose cried out then, a piercing wail of agony. Panic coursed through Lise.

Simon started too, as though he could see what was in Lise's heart, as though her fear brought him back from his own private hell. He moved toward them as though awakening from a nightmare. His shoulders straightened as he moved and his jaw hardened.

"You can do this, Lise," he said, crouching beside her, his eyes blazing with confidence.

Lise squeezed Rose's hand. She had to be able to do this. For Rose. For the baby. She swallowed hard and took a deep breath. For herself.

"Find out when her pains started," she instructed.

Simon turned to Rose and spoke in rapid pidgin English.

Rose's response was high and frightened. Lise squeezed her hand again to reassure her.

"Her contractions began around lunch time," Simon said. "They were very light so she decided to carry on working."

Rose cried as she spoke, her tears mingling with the dust on her cheeks.

Lise placed her hand on the young woman's belly. Like a band of steel, a contraction tightened the flesh beneath her fingers. Lise glanced at her watch and began to time the contraction.

"They've built her a birthing hut," Simon translated. "She wants to go there. She wants John to go away. He's not supposed to see her in labor. The people have a lot of traditions around birthing." His voice dropped even lower. "A lot of taboos. Men are not allowed." He looked at Lise. "Can we move her?"

God knows, she would like to. She would like to hand the young woman over to some experienced village midwife who wouldn't tread on tribal customs, who wouldn't make a mistake.

"No," Lise answered, silently counting off the seconds of the next contraction. "We can't move her. Her contractions are only a minute apart."

Rose's moans became a steady crescendo of agony. John paced uncertainly at the edge of the clearing, casting longing looks at the path through the trees. Rose grabbed Lise's hand and choked out a few words. Simon answered the laboring woman, his voice low and soothing. Lise looked at him, waiting.

"I told her we can't move her. She wants John sent away."

"Do it then," Lise said.

Simon barked an order over his shoulder and, with a single backward glance, John ran off. "I told him to go to my house and get some blankets and towels," Simon said, grinning at Lise, the tension in his face softening. "That should keep him out of the way for a while."

"What about you? Is she objecting to you being here?" Lise couldn't quite hide the tremor in her voice.

"Of course," Simon said, smiling. "But I told her you need me—"

Lise's shoulders stiffened. She didn't want to need him.

"—to translate."

His smile melted a portion of the fear threatening to overwhelm her. "Good," was all she said, but she could hear the relief in her own voice. She turned back to Rose and began to gently massage the woman's taut stomach, hoping Rose's muscles would relax and let the contractions work effectively.

Rose shrieked again, a heart-stabbing sound that rent the tranquil air and prickled Lise's skin. She glanced at Simon. A suggestion of the pain she had seen earlier flickered in his eyes, but the man she knew was back along with his strength. He had fought his private demons and was again in control.

"I have to examine Rose," Lise said, her eyes feeling over-dry and itchy. Heaven only knew what taboos she'd be breaking.

Rose's body dripped with sweat, yet her hands

and feet, when Lise touched them, were cold as ice. She was already in transition, Lise realized, but something was wrong. There seemed to be more than the usual amount of discomfort. She lifted the front of Rose's laplap. Gently, carefully, Lise examined her. Ten centimeters already. The cervix was fully dilated. Then she sucked in a sharp breath. A cervical lip remained and already Rose was straining to push.

It was difficult to get a good view. Lise leaned closer to the ground. Simon touched her on the shoulder, warming her, encouraging her. She placed her hand on Rose's abdomen and watched during the next contraction.

The baby's head was crowning. Excitement filled Lise's chest, then just as swiftly died. This wasn't the head. The baby's tiny bottom showed for an instant, then was sucked back up the birth canal at the end of the contraction.

The heat drained from Lise's face. "It's a breech!" she said quietly, not wanting Rose to know by expression or tone, just how serious that was.

"What does that mean," Simon asked.

"Bottom first," Lise whispered. "Difficult, even dangerous, in a hospital, but out here!" She gazed around despairingly. "Perhaps impossible."

"You can do it, Lise," Simon said, his steady voice reassuring.

She glanced again at the young woman straining with the pressure of a baby who wanted out. She had to do it. Rose had no one else.

The young woman panted rapidly, her eyes shutting each time a contraction hit her. She disappeared into her own world of sensation, her body embarking on its own rhythm.

Lise was awed by the strength and single-mindedness of Rose's laboring body. The contractions rocking her were intense, but she rode them as a surfer would ride a wave. Lise did what she could to help, panting rhythmically with the young woman, accompanying her on her ride.

The baby seemed determined to fight its way out, but Lise didn't dare let Rose push yet. The cervical lip was just enough to impede the baby. If it swelled with the added pressure of pushing, things would become more difficult than they already were.

Rose seemed to have forgotten Simon was there, but Lise hadn't. His presence centered her, strengthened her, pervaded her being so that her hand was his hand too. They were joined together in aiding the most wondrous journey this baby would ever make.

When she checked the cervix again, the lip was gone. It was time for Rose to push now. Lise pulled a bottle of disinfectant from her bag and poured it over her hands.

"Ready?" she asked, smiling faintly as she met Simon's eyes.

He nodded, his gaze never leaving hers.

"She can't deliver lying down like this. Gravity would help. Go behind her, Simon. Support her in a squatting position." Lise was amazed at how different she felt. Her voice was firm. She knew what she had to do.

Simon linked his arms under Rose's arms, supporting her as directed. "Now what?"

"Hold her, Simon. Keep her upright. Let her rest on you between contractions. She's going to need all her strength she can muster to get this little one out."

As she looked at Simon, Lise's heart contracted. He held Rose with the gentleness he would give a child, yet his face was set and determined. He ran his tongue over his lips as if to moisten them, then whispered encouragement to Rose, his tone giving an illusion of softness where there was only strength.

Lise breathed rhythmically in and out. She found Rose's pattern and helped the laboring woman keep it. Together, they mustered strength between the contractions.

Rose's abdomen tightened, released, then tightened again. Lise sucked in a deep, cleansing breath, then let it go. She locked her gaze on Rose's, willing the young woman to breathe in the same manner. Together, they sucked in another breath. Rose didn't need an example now. She held the next breath, pushing through it. Her body knew what it had to do.

While Rose strained, Lise massaged the opening through which the baby was struggling. With her other hand, she pressed down gently on Rose's belly.

Three difficult pushes and the baby's bottom was out.

Lise shot a quick glance at Simon. The wonder in his eyes raised goosebumps on her arms. He smiled broadly, as though some terrible load had been eased from his shoulders.

"It's a boy," he whispered.

"Give me your shirt!" Lise said hurriedly. "If the baby's bottom feels cold, he could try to breathe. And it's too soon for that."

Simon loosened his hold on Rose one arm at a time and shrugged out of his shirt. He tossed it to Lise and she wrapped the baby's bottom in it, then, gently, brought first one of the baby's legs down and free, then the other. She briefly touched the umbilical cord, rejoicing in its strong, clear pulse.

She supported the baby's body in both hands, her thumbs meeting along its back and her fingers stretching evenly over its pelvis and thighs. Slowly, she pulled him downward, then upward, all the while murmuring encouragement to Rose.

The baby's arms were flexed across his chest. One at a time, Lise drew them out.

Now the head.

Lise took a shallow breath. Rose was handling the difficult labor amazingly well. Although the young highland woman hung from Simon's arms, it was not from weakness. She seemed to realize she had to preserve her strength. She seemed to know they were on her side.

The baby's back faced upward. Lise lowered its body until she could see the nape of its neck. Tightly curled black hair sprung out along the edge of the cervical opening.

She swept her arm under the baby and hooked her fore and middle fingers into his mouth, bringing his chin down so that it rested on his neck, fully flexing the baby's head.

She placed her other hand over the baby's shoulder and placed two fingers on either side of its neck.

Gently . . . gently, she pulled as Rose pushed, lifting the baby in an upward arc as she did so. The nose and the mouth came free, but Lise pulled very slowly, knowing it was dangerous for the baby's head to pop out suddenly.

There. It was over.

Lise rotated the tiny body laying in her hands and gently cleaned its mouth and nose. The newborn's cry filled the air. A soft sigh escaped Lise's lips. Tears of joy slid down her cheeks. She glanced up at Simon, longing to share her happiness with him.

He was staring at the child as though it were a miracle. And it was. She couldn't bear for this to end, this perfect miracle in this perfect place. She smiled at Simon.

With this perfect man.

Then her chest burned and her mouth went dry. She loved Simon. Loved. The very word was terrifying. Yet wonderful. Too enormous to contain. She couldn't look at it now. She couldn't open wide her heart and examine what was there. There was still too much to do. It was enough to know the love was waiting there, sustaining her, nourishing her.

She gently laid the baby in its mother's arms and cut the umbilical cord, longing to hold the baby boy forever, to rejoice as she stroked his brand-new skin and perfect limbs.

But he wasn't hers to keep. The joy on Rose's face made it easier to relinquish him. Quietly, she asked Simon to lower the young mother to the ground.

Rose was beautiful. Bathed with perspiration, limp with exhaustion; none of that mattered. Nothing could diminish this moment of connecting to her new little son. She tucked her child's body into her arms and offered him her breast. With a lusty, slurping sound, he suckled. For an instant, Rose tore her gaze away and glanced at Lise, pride and gratitude shining from wide brown eyes.

Lise grinned back, happiness warming her like a blanket of sunshine. This was what life was about. She looked at Simon. This ultimate joy shared with someone you loved.

As soon as Rose had delivered the placenta, Lise spread the young woman's laplap over her and the baby. The new mother shut her eyes, already close to sleep. It was what she most needed now: gentle, healing sleep.

Lise sat back on her heels and scooped up a handful of earth. She let it run through her fingers, spilling into a pyramid below. Warm earth, nurturing, the perfect bed.

Simon's hand caressed her shoulder. She

looked up the lean length of him, up into the welcome of his eyes. He held out his hand and brought her to her feet, his strength bolstering hers.

A power filled her. A power strong enough to tackle the world and everything in it. Simon's eyes shone with pride. Lise's lip trembled. The pride was for her.

He pulled her to him in an explosive hug, comforting, rewarding, but with a promise of something different, something much more wonderful. She could have stood there forever. Not talking, not even thinking. Simply feeling.

She rested against the circle of his arms and gazed up into his face. His lips lowered to hers, warm and pulsing with life, just like the baby they had helped deliver. How could she ever have thought he was cold? Or hard? He was neither.

He kissed her thoroughly, then drew away. "You did it," he said, smiling down at her.

"Rose did it," Lise corrected. "We only helped."

"You dared." There was a happiness about him she hadn't seen before, a sparkle to his eyes, a lightening of his shoulders. It seemed a joy beyond what the birth had brought. It almost hid the remnants of pain in his eyes.

"What was it, Simon?" He hadn't answered when she had asked him before. The urgency of the birth had swept all else before it. She took his hand. "What troubled you before?"

He took a step backward and glanced down at Rose. The sight of her sleeping, her baby in her arms, reassured him somehow. If he could hang on to that, to the joy of the birth, he could keep the pain at bay.

"It doesn't matter now." If he kept himself safe, it need never matter again.

Lise stepped toward him and grasped his arm. "You told me to face things, Simon. You told me not to run away."

The tips of her fingers pressing into his skin should have been painful, but he felt nothing. It was as though his body had already grown numb. He could make his mouth move, but no sound emerged. He took one breath, then another, the first not nearly satisfying. Lise looked stricken, but she could not possibly know.

"Tell me," she whispered. "Tell me."

He shut his eyes, praying the resulting blackness would smother the image of Marion's face when she had told him. Would take away the memory of her pale eyes watching him coldly, studying him as she did her subjects, impartial, uncaring.

Anger flew up his throat in a sickly thrust and erupted into the words he had learned to subdue. "My wife was pregnant!"

Lise's eyes were wide.

"She had an abortion." The word still shocked him, sickened him, when referring to his own wife, his own baby. It was as though his life had seeped from his body, as his baby had left his wife's, leaving him cold and alone.

Lise's fingers tightened around his arm. She seemed unaware of it, frozen, linked to him with an unbreakable grasp. But nothing was unbreakable. He'd learned that much from Marion.

"She planned it, arranged it, went through with it." If he spat out the words, purged them from his body like the poison they were, perhaps finally he'd be free.

"But when she told you—"

"I didn't know about the abortion until it was all over." It felt now as it had then, like a blow to the stomach knocking out his wind. Marion's face had been flushed when she had told him, with a modicum of guilt and a bushel of relief. Nowhere had he seen regret, nowhere had he seen the agony threatening to fell him.

"Why?" Lise whispered.

That same question had reverberated endlessly

from one side of his brain to the other, dulling him, mocking him, filling him with pain.

"She didn't love me," he answered, believing it now as he hadn't at the time. "Wanted no part of what we had together, including the baby. She knew I wanted a child."

He fought back the rage threatening to explode. "If only I'd known she would do what she did."

"How could you have known?"

"By having the eyes to see. I've got them now."

Her grip loosened then, slowly, as if her hand had clutched his arm for so long and with such intensity it was frozen into place, as if it hurt her to uncurl her fingers and stretch them straight.

"Did Marion say she didn't want a baby?"

Nerves jumped in places he hadn't known existed. "No," he said wearily. "She didn't say that."

With a tentative gesture, Lise touched his arm again, running her palm over the surface of his skin, smoothing out the indents her nails had made.

"And I didn't ask. If I had, it needn't have ended the way it did. Needn't have started."

"But you said you wanted the baby."

He brushed a hand over his eyes. "More than

my life. But I was wrong in assuming she did, too." His chest ached with loathing, at himself now more than Marion. "Maybe I didn't listen hard enough. Maybe I hoped a baby would fill the gaping holes in our marriage. I've thought about it endlessly and I just don't know.

"The only thing I do know is it needn't have happened. If she had been honest with me, if I had been honest with myself, our baby wouldn't have died."

"Your baby's death was not your fault," Lise protested.

He grabbed her by the shoulders, needing to touch her, needing her warmth. Hating his need.

"She lied to me!" As women did. As Lise had, too. He released her shoulders with a jerk, wanting to fling her away, barely able to let her go. "And I lied to myself which is just as bad."

Lise stood tall before him, not looking like Marion, not acting like Marion, but . . .

Simon swallowed hard. "It's not a mistake I'm going to make again." He touched her cheek. "I'm sorry, Lise, but I can't do this."

Her withdrawal was more than a physical retreat. Her skin tightened paper thin across her face and her chest rose and fell in a staccato beat. But it was the sound that almost destroyed him.

A sound which was silent yet echoed in his ears. A snapping, a groaning, a shifting, a crunching, like one iceberg rubbing against the other until its shape changed irrevocably.

The sound of two hearts breaking at once.

Chapter Eleven

Connor glanced at her reproachfully as he swept the dirt from the floor of the haus sik into the dustpan. The ache in Lise's chest just wouldn't go away and the look on Connor's face made her throat constrict with shame. She hadn't heard a word he had said and it wasn't the first time her mind had been off on a whirligig of hopes, dreams, confusion and despair.

She focused on Connor's lips.

"We're going to the Baiyer River Bird Sanctuary," he said again, his eyes alive with excitement. "Next Sunday. Can you come?"

"Come?" she repeated.

"Yes." His voice was impatient.

"I'm sure your uncle would rather the two of you go alone."

"But he said to ask you."

She stooped and examined his face. "Your uncle Simon said to ask me?" Hope flickered through her body, erupting into a fierce pounding of her heart.

"Yes. He said I could bring a friend and I chose you."

"Oh." The flicker died faster than it had come to life. She struggled to hide the pain.

"I'm sorry, Connor," she said gently, not wanting to hurt him, liking him more than she could allow herself to show. "I'll be busy that day. I promised my aunt I'd help her at the Vocational Center. Her students are away on term break and we've got all the garden work to keep up."

The dejection in his eyes was unbearable, but she couldn't be where Simon was, not feeling as she did. Couldn't get any more attached to Connor, either. It would hurt the boy too much when she left New Guinea. It would hurt her, too.

She ruffled his hair and smiled at him. Then she stood and stared out the open door. Nobody in sight.

It had been two long weeks since Simon had last driven up that drive. Two lonely, unendurable weeks. Why had she fallen in love with a man who couldn't return that love?

She rolled her shoulders, laboring to unknot the tension lingering in her back. She had been working too hard, using work to erase the agony in her heart. But she was tired. Dead tired. She glanced back at the clock. Just mid-afternoon, but she would close up early for once.

The serrated-edged leaves of the banana tree in front of the building suddenly lifted like a grass skirt in the wind. Lise shivered. A cloud had formed overhead, obliterating the sun and with it the heat of the day.

A real storm was rolling in, not just the regular Monsoon rains, but a proper roof-raising, river-flooding tropical storm. She shivered again and went back inside.

Connor was shrugging into a too-long pullover. It hung down over his shorts, his skinny, little-boy knees sticking out like knobs on a door.

Lise had to fight hard to hold back her tears. It was one thing to protect herself from Simon, but Connor . . . She rubbed the moisture from her eyes. She couldn't let him go home so sad.

"Connor!"

The short-wave radio in the corner erupted into action. Crackling, screeching and popping, it seemed possessed with a life of its own. Brother Michael had shown her how to work it, but she hadn't expected to ever have to. Why weren't the brothers picking up the receiver on their set? It crackled again, urging her to answer. She lifted the receiver and depressed the talk button.

"Hello. Over," she said, disliking the idea of

her voice being flung helter-skelter over the airwaves, fetching up heaven only knew where.

She listened carefully to the voice on the other end.

"Yes, Father Philip, I understand," she answered, a chill settling over her body. How on earth was she going to get to Kol? It was in the middle of the Jimi Valley, miles away from anywhere. According to Father Philip, a storm had made the roads impassable, probably the same storm now spreading across the Wahgi valley.

She pulled over a pad of paper and wrote down the details. "You can count on me," she said, taking a deep breath. "I'll be there as quickly as I can. Over."

She placed the receiver back in its cradle, opened the louvered windows and peered out. Dark sheets of rain pelted from the clouds, frothing like tidal waves along the hill bordering the station. Within minutes the school itself would be drowning in floods from the sky. She picked up the telephone.

"Is your uncle home?" she asked Connor, dialing Simon's number as she spoke.

Connor's brows rose as high as his hairline. "He should be in his office," the boy said in his childish treble.

"Hello?" came Simon's deep impatient bass

into her ear.

She couldn't seem to talk.

"Hello," he repeated irritably.

"Simon, it's me."

"What is it?"

"Can you fly me into the Jimi?" She twined the telephone cord around her fingers as she asked the question.

"When?" Impersonal, cold.

"Now."

"Now!" he exploded.

Lise held the phone away from her ear, then gingerly returned it.

"Look out the window, woman," Simon said more softly.

"Later might be too late," she said. "Father Philip called. A young man has been badly injured in a bride price ceremony."

"How?"

"A pig attacked him." She could hear the disbelief in her own voice. New Guinea pigs were not the pink, curly-tailed, garden variety that were found in the Western world, but she had difficulty visualizing one attacking anybody, let alone a full grown man.

"They can be vicious if they're riled," Simon said flatly, "especially with the men. They don't feed them or take care of them, don't know how to handle them as the women do."

"So will you do it?"

"It would be insane to take a plane out in this kind of weather, especially at this time of day." His voice sounded like thunder. "The place will be socked in with clouds. You need good visibility to get into the Jimi."

"But will you do it?" she asked, her heart thudding against the wall of her chest. The idea of flying in his airplane again, buffeting from one cloud to the next, filled her with terror.

"It's too dangerous." There was a long silence. "You could be killed. I can't take that risk."

A dry laugh rattled her throat. "Risk! You're afraid of the risk? I thought the only thing you were afraid to risk was your heart."

"If you're so determined to help," he snapped, "I'll fly in, get the fellow, and bring him to you."

"What if he can't be moved? You won't be able to assess that. I have to go."

He swore, a brief and highly colorful expletive.

"Simon!"

"Meet me at the airstrip in twenty minutes. We'll see."

~*~

Simon stood by his plane, his lean, angular

body braced stoically against the driving rain and blasting wind. Lise clutched her medical case and tried to still the flutters in her stomach. Her curls whipped in front of her face, then settled wetly across her cheek. Impatiently, she flung them back, slammed shut the door of her aunt's car, and moved toward Simon.

He uncurled gracefully from beneath the wing, displeasure evident in every taut line. His brown cords clung to the muscular contours of his thighs. His broad shoulders seemed larger than ever trapped in the chocolate-colored leather of his jacket.

His eyes were black granite beneath the glowering crag of his brow. He ran his hand over the afternoon stubble on his chin. In the opaque light of the darkening sky, Lise quailed at the grim set of his lips.

"I thought you'd never ride with me again?"

"I thought so, too. But I have no choice."

"You don't need to do this, Lise."

"Yes, I do. And I need you to help me." Faster than a heartbeat, she added the one thing she prayed he couldn't resist, "I dare you."

Had she miscalculated? She searched his face anxiously, expecting and dreading resistance. Instead, a smile began slowly, then spread like lightning across his face. His teeth gleamed against the storm's gloom. With the grace of a cat, he shook his wet hair from his face and laughed. Then he reached for her hand and squeezed her fingers.

"Well, Dr. Dawson," he said, "you'd better get in." He took her bag, threw it behind the passenger seat, then helped her up the slippery metal step.

She was actually doing it. She was entering this devil's plaything in the most vicious weather imaginable. She had concentrated so hard on getting Simon to take her, she'd been able to ignore her fear. Now it swept back stronger than ever.

The only thing moving her forward into the cockpit was the warmth of Simon's hand on her back and the knowledge that an injured man waited. She breathed in a shaky breath, afraid her legs would give way and she would end up in an ignominious heap on the grass runway.

With a boost from Simon, she tumbled into her seat, the door clanging shut behind her. No turning back now. She fumbled for her seat belt, aware the flimsy strap would provide little protection in the event of a crash.

She peered through the window, unable to see a thing with the rain streaming across the glass. She swallowed hard and closed her eyes, momentarily blocking out both the wind and the rain. It was even worse with her eyes shut. Too many frightening images coursed through her brain. With a sigh, she opened them again.

In this weather, a crash seemed inevitable. She'd been insane to push Simon into this.

He unfastened the ropes anchoring the plane to the ground, flung open the door and climbed in beside her. Now there was no room at all. Every inch of space was taken with the bulk of a very wet, very unpredictable male.

His shoulder rubbed against hers, setting her nerve endings ablaze. She drank in the smell of him: his hair fresh and fragrant like grass after a summer's shower; his soaked leather jacket, pungent and evocative of basic animal instincts; his skin musky, yet soap-clean, warmed with an inner heat, yet touched with the pureness of rain.

"Ready?" he asked, gazing at her appraisingly.

She nodded, unable to trust her voice. She placed her hands on her lap, determined not to clutch at her seatbelt.

Simon began flipping the labeled switches in front of him so quickly she could hardly tell where his hands had been and where they were going next. First the fuel, then the magnetos, then the master—master of what? Finally, the starter. The propeller turned, there was a puff of smoke, and the plane rocketed with sound, almost covering the din of the storm outside.

The plane began to move. It wobbled and bounced down the runway as steadily as a teacup in a hurricane, gusts of wind rocking it from side to side. They gradually gathered speed, the windshield wipers working overtime.

Simon fought the aircraft's nose into the wind, then pulled slowly back on the half-wheel. The plane lifted.

Lise abandoned her resolve and braced herself against her seat as the earth dropped sickeningly beneath them. Simon switched off the wipers, the rain now blowing off the windshields faster than it could drop.

As the plane climbed, Lise peered out into the storm. For a moment or two, the sky seemed lighter, then Simon banked the aircraft to the right and headed into the thickest, darkest cloud she had ever seen.

"Damn!"

"What is it?" she whispered.

His face was disturbingly close. He blinked as though to clear his eyes, and his thick full eyelashes brushed against his cheeks.

"Can't see a bloody thing," he growled, peering out the window again.

"Can't you fly by instruments, radar or something?"

He gave a mirthless laugh. "I don't have radar. Wouldn't do us much good anyway. We're not flying above the mountains."

"We're not?"

"We go through them. We have to find the gap into the Jimi."

Lise swallowed hard. "What if we can't see?"

"Exactly." His lips tightened. "It's not too late to turn back."

"No."

"Good girl," he said, smiling fleetingly at her.

Rapidly, they approached the dark hills surrounding the long and narrow Jimi Valley. It seemed to Lise as though her stillness was unnatural compared to Simon's constant movement. One hand held tight to the steering yoke while his other on the throttle worked the engine to its limit. His gaze alternated constantly from the map clipped to the steering mechanism to the ground below.

Lise peered at the map herself but could make no sense of the tiny lines and squiggles. She could only sit and pray they would get out of this safely. She had no control at all anymore. Not over her life—she stole a glance at Simon—or over her heart.

Then the plane dropped out from under her and when she fell back into her seat, it was with a spine-jarring thump. There was no time to breathe, no time to grab hold, before they were bounced into another air pocket like a rubber dingy down a rapid.

Both of Simon's hands were on the controls now, working hard to keep the aircraft steady. The plane swooped and soared, wings dipping and rising.

"There!" Simon shouted, pointing to a barely visible gap between the mountains. Clouds clung to the sides of the gap like barnacles to a ship's bottom.

The rain drove down as fiercely as ever, hurting Lise's ears with its deafening roar.

"Can we make it through?" she shouted. "Is there space below those clouds?"

"There has to be." His lean fingers gripped the controls with confidence.

He did everything confidently. Perhaps that's what kept him safe. What seemed insane risk-taking to her was simply a challenge to him, a well-calculated exercise in determining what was possible. Perhaps she should stop worrying so much and simply trust the man.

She kept her focus on him, and gradually, the courage prompting her to venture on this mission of mercy was replenished by his strength. Her trembling slowed along with her breathing. Everything would be all right. She had to believe that.

Then they entered the gap.

"Hang on!" Simon yelled above the roar of the engine.

Lise's gaze was pulled to the clouds clinging to the sides of the pass. They seemed to expand and drift downward in a black miasma of evil. Lise's lungs cried out for oxygen, but if she opened her mouth to breathe, the black mist might engulf them.

Lower and lower they plunged, tossed like a leaf on the currents of air sweeping through the passage. Jagged rocks loomed on either side, rocks so close she could have reached out and touched one. With one wing toward the ground, they barely squeaked through.

Then, as suddenly as they entered the pass, they were out the other side.

Lise breath came out in a rush. She wrenched her gaze from the sharp points of rock threatening to rip their aluminum bird from stem to stern and looked back at Simon instead.

"Still with me?" he yelled.

"Yes!" she cried. Even with the danger, even with her concern over the injured man awaiting her help, she could feel the excitement, the relief of staring danger in the eye and winning. Maybe this was why Simon took the risks he took. Maybe this was why he dared.

Then, without warning, an ethereal glow surrounded them. The trees disappeared and the out-juttings of rocks were gone. No, not gone. She just couldn't see them through the mist descending from nowhere.

Though the mist was filled with moisture, Lise's mouth felt filled with cotton batting. The heat drained from her face, the relief from her heart. Her hand stole out and landed on Simon's thigh. Just touching him, feeling the warmth of his body, made it possible to suppress the scream battering against her lips.

Simon pushed forward on the wheel, his face ashen. He edged the plane lower, ever lower, toward trees capable of piercing its fragile shell.

This time when she held her breath, her lungs expanded to the limit. For what seemed an eternity, the ground became only too visible as it raced toward them like a slamming door.

Simon swerved to avoid the trees, his entire body in motion. His hands worked the controls, his feet worked the rudder pedals, his gaze was everywhere: on the map, on the swiftly approaching ground, and then suddenly, briefly, on Lise herself.

The warmth in his eyes, the familiarity, the oneness, prompted an unaccustomed sensation to undulate through her body. From the center of her being, it swept in all directions: toward her knees, rendering them useless; toward her chest, resulting in such a fervent pounding of her heart she was sure Simon would not only hear it but would go deaf from the din; and toward her head, swimming with images.

"We'll make it yet," Simon said. And then he smiled, a slow, sensuous, heart-stopping sort of smile.

"I know," whispered Lise, suddenly sure of it, trusting him as she had never trusted anyone before.

Simon's gaze flickered from her face to the ground below. Lise duplicated his scrutiny, her brows drawing together.

"We can't be more than a hundred feet up!" she exclaimed. And dropping rapidly. "We're too low, Simon!"

Though his face was attentive, he said nothing.

She clamped her lips together, determined to keep her faith. They dropped further, eighty feet, sixty, fifty.

Some of the trees were as high, but still the

mist pushed them lower.

"Simon!" she cried, his very name a protest.

"We don't need ten feet, or even five," he said, giving her a flashing, brilliant grin, his eyes very dark and bright. "A foot is all we need if we're pressed."

Lise squeezed her eyes shut, unable to watch his face as he played leapfrog with death. She counted the beats of her heart, as an insomniac would sheep, prepared to try anything, do anything, to keep her mind off the danger. But her heart beat too quickly. She lost track, couldn't keep up.

"Lise," Simon said, his voice coming at her as if through a tunnel. "Are you sleeping again?" The relief in his voice penetrated the barrier she had clamped over her eyes and mind.

Cautiously, she opened her eyes.

"There's the road to Karap," he said, pointing to a thin, red line below them. "Just past Karap is Kol."

The mercurial mist had disappeared as suddenly as it had come. They were higher again, safer. Lise breathed in deeply, her heartbeat slowing. She had prepared herself for death at Simon's side, but they might just make it.

Below them was the jungle, a blanket of leafy green as impenetrable to sight as fabric. But out of the lushness rose a butte, and on the butte stood a pandanus tree, its sword-like leaves a stark sentinel against the sky. Lise's throat tightened. She'd never seen anything so beautiful, so strong.

"The country's working its magic on you," Simon said.

She nodded, unable to speak. He stared at her for a long moment, as though he saw something in her eyes he hadn't expected to see. Then a muscle rippled along his jaw and he turned his face away. She turned also, trying not to feel.

The airstrip was in sight, a too-short slash in the jungle. They swooped in over the trees and dropped into position. Simon cut the power and lowered the nose of the plane toward the edge of the grassy runway. He maneuvered left, then right, raised the nose to flare, then, in a gentle stall, fluttered the plane to the ground with scarcely a bump. They rattled down the landing strip and came to a halt ten feet from the end.

The engine's whine died, but nothing could silence the turmoil in Lise's heart.

Chapter Twelve

Lise ducked low to enter the hut, blinded for an instant by the blackness and choked by the smell of blood. She peered toward the back of the hut, at the figures huddled around the injured man. Simon pressed in behind her, forcing her forward to where the feather-bedecked figure of the headman kneeled next to the injured man. It was the headman who had insisted the young man be brought into the hut, the headman who had decreed the spirits were better there for healing. Judging from his close scrutiny of her, the headman wasn't taking any chances on offending the spirits.

Lise's fingers were slick with sweat, her medical bag unbearably heavy in her hand. She reviewed its contents in her mind, worried she had left something out, something she would need, something that would make the difference between success and failure.

Then, suddenly, the injured man groaned and she dropped to her knees at his side. Blood. Red blood. Like her father's had been red when his life had seeped away. It dripped from the young man's leg to the mat beneath him, drying at the edges of the wound into a red-black crust. The two women caring for the wounded man had tried to staunch the blood's flow by stuffing the wound with mud and leaves, but had been unsuccessful. They gazed expectantly at Lise.

The heat drained from her face and for one excruciating moment, she was sure she would faint. She pressed her eyes closed to shut out the blood, but the memory of it, the smell of it, the whirring of the flies attracted by its presence, didn't go away.

Simon's hand touched her shoulder. She bit hard on her bottom lip and forced her eyes open, then unlatched her bag and drew out her things, forcing herself to examine the wound, willing herself not to falter.

She cleared away the poultice the villagers had applied, sluicing the dirt away with water, then liberally pouring antiseptic into the wound. A quiet word, a swift glance and, one by one, Simon handed her the things she asked for. She cleaned and mended, relieved when she succeeded in staunching the flow of blood. She pulled the severed muscles and the edges of skin together and stitched them up. By the time she had drawn the needle through the young man's thigh for the last time, her hand was steady.

Simon was across from her now. He shifted his body to allow what little daylight was left to filter in through the low doorway and illuminate the wound.

"Is he going to make it?" he asked.

"Yes," Lise answered, not looking at Simon, not daring to do so.

From the moment they had first met, she had fought the attraction gripping her now. He was too bold, she had thought then, too daring, too dangerous. But he had given her his strength, and just as she was becoming whole, he had taken her heart.

Tears blurred her eyes. It wasn't her heart he wanted. It was her expertise, a doctor for his damned hospital. He had never told her he loved her.

Pain stabbed her chest as sharply as if it had been done with the needle in her hand. It was all very well to pretend not to love, but she did love and that was harder by far than the mending of bodies.

She flexed her tight shoulders. They ached from crouching awkwardly during the long repair process. Her legs were numb from lack of movement. She ran a practiced eye over the young man's leg. She had done all she could. He'd be fine, given a little time and modern antibiotics. She wished she could say the same about herself.

She rose stiffly and crawled out of the hut, knowing Simon was following, but not daring to look back. A single glance into his black eyes and she'd be lost forever.

The light outside dazed her. Then a steadying hand grasped her elbow, Simon's hand, and a sea of brown eyes came into focus. The entire village seemed to be waiting for news. They gazed expectantly, first at the headman who'd followed Simon out, then at Lise.

Her lips formed a smile, then she felt her body sway, swamped by the emotion of the afternoon and the impossibility of her love. Simon's grip tightened. It was unendurable. She wanted his touch, longed for his touch, but not like this. To be close to the man she loved, yet to deny that love, was torture of the worst kind.

She swiped away the perspiration on her forehead. She would have to leave New Guinea, not in a few months time as she had planned, but as soon as she could get a flight.

Whoosh. The broad blade of an ax head swung in front of Lise's nose. She stepped back hastily, bumping into Simon, then flinched forward again, like one bumper car hitting another, reluctant to lean on him, to need him, when soon she would have to leave him.

The headman paced in front of her, his ax arcing high, his arms and legs moving to the rhythm of his oration. Strong in spite of his years, the old man's voice rose and fell in the compelling cadence of a leader speaking to his people.

It was impossible to tell from the headman's tone if he was grateful for her efforts or upset with their intervention and modern ways. Brother Michael's stories of the people's anger when things went wrong filled her with dread.

"You're a hit, Dr. Dawson," Simon whispered, his warm breath caressing her ear.

"Wha . . .t do you mean?" she stammered, facing him at last. A current, as sharp as electricity, coursed between her body and his, disconcerting her, throwing her off balance. Then a warmth engulfed her, a warmth she would have to fight.

Simon nodded toward the people. The villagers presented a solid phalanx of warm brown skin and colorful Bird of Paradise feathers. Gathered to celebrate a wedding until the accident with the pig had forced a halt, they were still dressed in full ceremonial regalia.

The men held spears and bows and arrows and were as menacing as an oncoming army.

The women wielded the sharp digging sticks that accompanied them everywhere. But when Lise stared into their rain-drenched faces all she saw now was gratitude.

With a final, high-pitched explosion of words, the headman faced Simon and Lise. His battle-worn face altered and his mouth creased into a wrinkled grin.

"They want us to the stay the night," Simon drawled, his words raising the hair along the back of Lise's neck.

His hand drifted from her elbow and landed possessively on her shoulder, jolting Lise's nerve-endings with a heart-wrenching shudder.

"Stay the night? But that's out of the question. My aunt—" She twisted around to meet his eyes. "Aunt Cecile will be beside herself with worry."

"Well, darling—"

Her heart leapt at his choice of words.

"—we don't have any other option. It'll be dark in about fifteen minutes."

It was true. The sun had already fallen behind the tree line. In the soggy clearing, the people clutched their arms around their bodies, obviously cold and anxious to gather comfortably around their evening fires.

"You may feel your honor is worth risking a

flight in the dark, but I know my limits."

He was teasing her but what he said was true. They wouldn't be going anywhere tonight. Beneath Simon's strong, warm fingers, her skin quivered.

"Don't look so stricken, darling."

There was that word again. How could he say it so lightly? How could he say it and not mean it?

"They'll give us something to eat and a bed for the night."

"I'm not worried about food."

"So it's the sleeping arrangements then?" His face loomed closer—close enough to kiss. "Don't forget, as far as they're concerned, we're wantoks, clansman." His lips slid into a smile. "We speak the same language."

Did they?

"We'll probably be sharing a hut." The idea obviously didn't bother him at all.

"Isn't there a men's hut? Brother Michael told me every village has one."

His smile spread into a grin. "I wouldn't think of leaving you alone. Who would protect you?"

"I don't need anyone to protect me."

"Maybe not in a nunnery, but out here . . ."

What he said was true. Lise stiffened, maintaining her composure with difficulty. "I expect you to stay on your own side."

"Of the bed?" he asked innocently.

"Of the hut!" she exclaimed. The fire within her would ignite if he came too close.

"Aiyai . . ." The kina shell through the headman's nose wobbled as he began to speak once more.

Simon replied in the same singsong fashion, his speech strangely stirring to Lise. The headman grinned, nodded, then walked through the gap opening up between his people.

Lise glanced questioningly at Simon. What had he agreed to now? Simon cupped his hand under her elbow and led her along in the wake of the old man.

"You must have really impressed them, sweetheart. While you've been doctoring away, they've been busy as beavers preparing a spanking new hut for us to sleep in. Not only that, they've invited us to a little celebration tonight."

"What kind of celebration?"

"A karim leg ceremony. Quite an honor to be asked. Not many westerners have seen it."

"What is it?" Her brow puckered. What was it Aunt Cecile had told her about the different ceremonies in the area?

Simon grinned down at her. "Impossible to describe. You'll just have to wait."

~*~

Lise groaned and wished she could loosen the button on her shorts. Still-steaming pig meat and piping hot kaukau lay on a large banana leaf in front of her. Gourds filled with pineapple, bananas, papaya and sugar cane clustered around the hot dishes. She couldn't eat another bite, yet still the food kept coming.

Simon sprawled next to her, leaning comfortably against the wall of the hut. It had been impossible to concentrate on the ceremonies at the feast with every nerve in her body acutely focused on the man beside her. He leaned toward her, his shoulder bumping hers. Her inner warning system sounded.

"They get pig meat like this only once or twice a year," he said, his whisper tickling her ear. "They'll probably eat it all week long."

"I feel ready to burst already," Lise moaned.

"It'll take more than a feast to make you plump," he said, surveying her figure with dancing eyes.

"I wouldn't bet on it," she replied, cursing the warmth stealing over her cheeks. He shifted closer and his side touched hers. The heat from his body was like a flame to a moth.

She leaned away, a lump forming in her

throat. If he saw how he affected her, she would lose her pride. And if she lost that, he'd have everything.

"The food will give you energy. You're going to need it. The karim leg ceremony will start as soon as they've finished eating." Simon's usually serious face was animated.

It seemed an eternity before the last of the villagers sat back satiated. The headman swallowed one final succulent morsel of pork then began to speak, his voice rising and falling expressively.

Simon, who understood the language, appeared fascinated, but the more Lise tried to focus on the old man's storytelling, the more desperate she became. She couldn't eliminate Simon from her sight or mind and she couldn't go on sitting next to him.

Just when she'd given up all hope the evening would end, the headman suddenly stood. He gestured for the others to do the same. Grinning toothlessly at Simon and Lise, he beckoned them to follow him.

"You have to explain—" The rest of Lise's words were lost as Simon grabbed her hand and pulled her with him out of the feasting hut, through the black night and driving rain, to the hut of the karim leg.

The headman gestured to the floor of the hut

where other unmarried couples formed a circle around the fire pit.

Swallowing convulsively, Lise moved to a shadowy corner and sat down next to Simon.

The headman leaned over a small pile of sticks and struck a match. He touched the flame to a piece of dry kindling and cupped his hand around it, keeping the draft from the door away until the fire had caught. Within moments, the fire blazed to life, the villagers drawing back from the heat.

Lise glanced at Simon. With the heat permeating her damp clothes and the shadows cloaking her face, she was beginning to feel relaxed. Too relaxed. She couldn't afford to let her guard down. Simon must never discover how she felt about him. Misery washed over her. Not if he didn't love her.

Her heart swelled at the sight of his stern profile, growing softer now with the play of firelight on the planes of his face. She tried to harden her heart, to look at him without imagining the joy of being with him forever, but it was impossible.

Resolutely, she averted her eyes. Simon took more risks than she liked, but that no longer mattered. His courage was a large part of what she loved about him. But he didn't want her; at least, not in the way she needed. A kiss, a cuddle, even a whole lot more was what he desired, but not a commitment; never a commitment.

"You're beautiful," Simon said, drawing her gaze back to his with a voice as soft as moonlight.

Words of love, but not the right words.

He brushed her hair back from her face. "Like silk," he murmured.

His touch moved her as an earthquake moves boulders. Need rumbled up from her center and exploded outward. She longed to shut her eyes, desperate to stem the tide of her desire. But it was impossible.

The liquid black of his eyes caressed and enticed her. Her breathing grew more rapid and her lips parted. She tried to pull away, but was drawn back as inexorably as a bee is to nectar.

Thump! The hollow sound reverberated throughout the hut, then sounded again as the headman palmed the drum once more.

"The Kundu drum," Simon whispered. "Said to contain all kinds of powers."

All talk died and the sound of the drum and of Simon's words sunk deep into Lise's bones. Electricity charged the air.

Then the headman ceased his playing and an expectant silence filled the air. Solemnly, the headman laid the Kundu drum beside the fire. Through the flames, his painted face was frightening.

Lise felt suddenly certain, with a premonition so intense her body shivered despite the heat, that there was magic in that drum.

In this hut.

In this night. She glanced again at Simon.

In this man.

The headman threw more wood on the fire, building it up until the flames were high and hot. In a rhythmic, hypnotic voice, he began to chant. He picked up a small gourd etched with black-and-white markings and drew from it a handful of powder. With great ceremony, he threw the powder on the fire.

Iridescent spirals of topaz, scarlet and green flared up in the flames and danced like sunlight reflecting off a rainbow. With difficulty, Lise tore her gaze away and turned toward Simon. The ebony depths of his eyes were soothing after the fire's flashing color. Deeper and deeper, she sunk within them.

She attempted to draw back, failed, then tried again.

At last, with a great effort of will, she succeeded, her chest heaving from the strain. The other men and women had now paired into couples and were seated facing each other, the fire and smoke casting their shadows skyward, their eerie shapes playing on the roof and sides of the hut.

The women's bare breasts glowed provocatively and the men's pig-greased skin glistened in the firelight. The villagers swayed to the resumed throb of the Kundu, their eyes wide and luminous, their sensual mouths parted in expectation.

A shiver shimmied the length of Lise's spine. Then, with a suddenness that made her jump, the headman began to sing an accompaniment to the drum. She didn't understand the words but Simon's eyes drew her back, the music becoming magic in her soul.

Slowly, falteringly at first, the young man next to the headman raised a flute to his lips. Its pure notes soared up and over the rhythm of the drum. Language barriers, cultural barriers, barriers that Lise had raised herself, all ceased to matter. There was only the music and the magic it wrought.

An energy, buoyant and tempestuous, pulsed around her. Like the Kundu, only more intense. It promised life, daring and full, and love, rich and passionate.

Understanding engulfed Lise, her blood

boiling within. All this could be hers, if only for one night.

A chanting, soft and low at first, then increasing in intensity, burst from the throats of the other couples. A song of laughter, of pleasure, of expectation.

Undeniable longings tore at Lise's own heart, and she faced Simon, faced the man she loved.

He pulled her close, and imitating the other couples and following the custom of the karim leg, lifted her legs so they went up and over his. His heat burned through his trousers, warming her bare skin. Gently, he stroked the length of her thigh, blazing the warmth to fire.

She leaned closer, her lips desperate for the touch of his. His own particular scent, part clean earth, part musk, enveloped her, dizzied and overwhelmed her. But the midnight of his eyes steadied her, pulled her in. Despite the beat of the Kundu and the company of others, Lise felt alone with Simon, alone with her love.

He draped one arm around her shoulder, gently easing her forward until her lips brushed his. There was no need to breathe. She was suspended in time.

Her breasts swelled beneath the cotton fabric of her blouse, her nipples becoming taut as she breathed in Simon's essence. Her legs melted against his body, gripping him hard in an effort to get close.

He placed his hands on her buttocks and pulled her to him, so close his manhood bulged against her, sending waves of desire from her head to her toes.

She entwined her fingers in his hair and pulled his face toward her waiting lips.

His scar marked his face with danger, but his eyes promised safety. When his lips touched hers, she drew him closer, until he was breast to chest, lips to lips, and heart to heart.

"Come with me," Simon whispered, his voice husky.

Lise ran her tongue over her swollen lips. A wordless nod was all she could manage. Other couples were leaving, also, the magic of the karim leg compelling free rein to their passion in the privacy of the night.

Slowly, breathlessly, Lise untangled her limbs from Simon's. Then she paused, afraid suddenly, to go on. But he rose to his feet and she rose too, glad he was there, glad that she loved him, and grateful that he had made her whole.

The headman played on as they stumbled past, his old voice tunelessly chanting an accompaniment to the Kundu. He swayed to the enchantment of the music, his eyes glazed.

As though filled with a sudden urgency, Simon swiftly drew Lise from the hut's smoky interior into the rain-drenched night. They raced past the row of silent huts toward the one the people had built for them. Simon pulled aside the entrance flap and they ducked inside.

The embers of a small fire glowed in the center of the hut, its smoke rising in a thin band to a ventilation gap in the roof. Past the fire, an elaborately woven sleeping mat was piled high with a colorful selection of quilts and pillows.

Only one bed, ready for two. Lise caught her breath. There would be no suggestion now of Simon sleeping on one side of the hut and herself on the other. His arms encircled her from behind. She closed her eyes, feeling him with her, beside her, a part of her. She was unable to see him, but she knew he was there.

His chin rested on her shoulder. His lips played with the lobe of her ear. Absorbedly, he kissed his way to her neck, delicious sensations emanating downward, along the path of his tongue.

He turned her around to face him. His eyes had never seemed so black, or so intent, like two deep tunnels leading straight to his soul. He showered kisses as soft as raindrops onto her lips, then his kisses increased in intensity until

Lise was not sure she was even breathing. Perhaps Simon was breathing for her.

His tongue demanded entrance to the recess of her mouth. Willingly, she met his tongue with hers, tasting him, savoring him.

He held her closer, caressing her back until she arched toward him. He lifted her blouse, freeing her skin to his touch. Heat followed in the path of his fingers as he explored the curves and contours of her back and sides. His hoarse groan vibrated against the hollow of her throat, then he swept her off her feet and into his arms.

He was a buccaneer, a daredevil, a gentleman all in one. He stared into her eyes, his scar white against his tan. Her pulse surged with the excitement and the danger, of being with him and loving him. Her heart pounded savagely, swelling with desire.

He skirted the fire and laid her squarely on the bed, then in a single fluid motion he was beside her, his lips never leaving hers. He unbuttoned her blouse, the fabric disappearing as if by magic. The rough warmth of his fingers caressed her breasts, lingering possessively on their satiny hills and valleys. The pounding of her heart was as fierce as the monsoon rains drumming in the puddles outside and on the roof above.

Lise closed her eyes, giving herself up to

sensation. Any inclination to deny had disappeared. She wished only to be enclosed by Simon's arms, to give herself to him, body and soul, if only for one night. For she loved this one-time stranger. She was prepared to take the risk.

He took her breast in his mouth, rolling the nipple between his lips, tantalizing it with his tongue. Moaning, Lise moved beneath him.

His hands traveled lower, unbuttoning the waistband of her shorts. He explored every inch of her, from her waist, to her belly, to the private place between her legs. A fountain of warmth swelled at his touch.

He rolled half on top of her, his powerful form molding itself to fit her curves. Exquisitely crushed beneath his muscular frame, she longed to be even closer. She pressed her body into his, gasping with need.

Feverishly, she unbuttoned his shirt and stroked his chest, poised on the pinnacle of an indescribably dizzy height, poised on the brink of giving everything she had.

Breathlessly, she submitted to her passion; the passion the drum had unleashed. Simon rose onto one elbow and, with a few impatient tugs, discarded his trousers. He stared down at her, his face just inches from her own, his eyes probing hers as though to satisfy himself of something.

For an instant, he turned away, away from Lise's gaze as she drank him in. The strong, clean lines of his throat and face were etched against the bright glow from the fire, and a longing grew within her such as she had never felt before.

Gently, she stroked his skin, from the tip of his determined chin along the vulnerable line of his throat. His pulse hammered against her finger and something in her responded fiercely to its message.

He turned back to her then, and smiled down at her, melting her body to liquid desire. His lips took hers hungrily, and he lowered himself onto her, his skin meeting hers in an explosion of heat.

He moved above her and filled her, body and soul, with the heady feast of love. They rocked together as the wind rocked the trees, her passion matching his. It was bigger than both of them, beyond their control.

It was magic.

Distantly, through the storm outside and the pleasure within, came the sound of the Kundu. Simon moved to its beat, thrusting into her again and again, until at last, with one long, shuddering sigh, he possessed her. The life force within her heard the beat and responded, opening to him as generously as the parched earth opens to the life-giving rain, until she too possessed.

Possessed the man she loved.

Chapter Thirteen

Eyes softly shut, a smile pulling the corners of her lips upward, Lise reached out for warmth. For Simon.

Her fingers came back empty.

Her eyelids flew open and she stared in disbelief at the empty spot on the bed beside her. The sheets, once warm with Simon's heat, were frigid. He had been gone for some time.

She struggled to a sitting position, rubbing her eyes to clear them. She glanced around the hut, seeking Simon, not finding him. His things were missing: his jacket, his bag.

He was gone.

Perhaps gone to get them something to eat. A clammy cold crept around Lise's heart. No, he wouldn't have taken his bag for that.

Shafts of sunlight danced through the cracks in the door flap, but the joy she had experienced the night before fled. Sick foreboding took its place.

She swallowed hard, tightening her lips to stop their quivering, willing herself not to cry. Last night had been perfect. Too perfect. And now it was over.

In the cold light of day, things were different. Perhaps Simon had remembered his wife and the way she had made him feel. He had loved his wife. Making love with an inexperienced stranger could never be the same. The magic she herself had felt was sure to be missing for him. He must have wakened beside her, stared down at her in horror, wondered how best to get out of this.

The easiest way had been to leave.

Lise reached for her opal, its surface now cold. It was supposed to have reminded her, supposed to have kept her safe. She had known Simon didn't love her. He had never said he did. He had been hurt too much to love.

Her breath came quickly, her naked breasts rising and falling, too exposed, too vulnerable. Desire still tightened her nipples, mocking her. She clutched the quilt to her neck, but Simon's scent rose from it faintly, bowling her over with the agony of loss. She curled into a tight ball of despair.

~*~

"Are you awake Lise?"

It was Simon. His voice. His warmth. Through swollen eyelids and frozen with dread, she squinted up into his face.

He kissed her lightly on the lips and desire shafted through her, so immediate and powerful, it shook her to her core. She wanted him too much. It hurt, wanting like that.

"I woke up and found you gone," she said softly, needing to remember how his absence had made her feel, terrified she would forget the deadening of her heart.

He kissed her again, sucking the breath from her body with the warm satin of his lips. "I had a few things to do," he said obliquely, his mouth moving against hers.

Her fear faded as he kissed her, was as elusive to hold on to as the wind. Unreliable happiness flowed in its stead. She tested it, ran her tongue across her lips and tasted it, reveled in it. Longing surged through her, too potent to put off.

"We should be going," he said hoarsely, his lips traveling up her cheek and across her temple.

Somewhere, on the outer reaches of her consciousness, she could hear the village stirring. An ax thudded dully against some wood. One child cried sharply to another.

Simon lifted his head and stared into her eyes. She touched his lips with her finger. Warm. She didn't want him to say anything. She didn't want the spell to break.

Not again. Not yet.

Desire lit his eyes. Groaning, he sat up. "We'd better get going, Lise. Your aunt will be worried." He caught her hand in his and rubbed it with his fingers. "Besides, we have a lot to do." He raised her hand to his lips and kissed it, too. "The contractor I hired is coming tomorrow to go over the hospital plans. I want you to see them first."

A chill came from nowhere and settled around her heart.

"See if they meet your approval."

The ice spread to her chest, rendering her stiff.

"You'll know best what you need."

Her breathing ceased. The only heat remaining was in her cheeks. He had made love to her to make her stay. He didn't want a wife. He wanted a doctor.

"There's no point in my looking through them," she said, biting her tongue to stop from crying out. "I won't be here when it's built."

His eyes turned so black it was as if the day had turned to night.

"Where will you be?" he growled.

She had to ignore the pain in his eyes. She

couldn't let it pull her in, fool her again.

"I start a job soon," she said, glancing at his lips and trembling. "Remember?"

He hurled himself from the bed. She couldn't see his face now, but from the way he stood, from the way he straightened his shoulders so stiffly, so angrily, she knew how it would look. The warmth would be gone and the soft lines would have hardened.

"You're leaving?"

The last vestige of hope died in her heart. If he loved her, he would have said so. If he loved her, he would never let her go.

"Yes."

"Right. I'll be waiting by the plane."

Without a backward glance, he ducked through the low doorway and left.

She stared at the doorway for a long time, unable to pull her gaze away. Maybe if she stared long enough, he'd come back through it and tell her the things she needed to hear. The things she couldn't live without. Tell her that he loved her.

"Lise." The voice came from outside the hut.

She clutched her quilt more tightly around her.

"It's Brother Michael." His voice was stiff with embarrassment.

"Brother Michael," she repeated, stunned.

"What are you doing here?" She grabbed her blouse, slid her arms into it and fumbled the buttons closed.

"Your aunt sent me."

Was his voice unnaturally loud or was it just the pounding in her head that made her wince?

"With the storm and everything, Cecile was worried about you."

Lise swung her legs from beneath the covers. She slid her shorts on and up, tucked in her blouse and looked around for her shoes. There they were, by the fire pit. Her legs worked. She slipped her feet into her shoes and in three short strides was at the door. She lifted the flap and ducked out into the clearing.

It was still early. Mist rose from the wet ground, the dew evaporating in the sun. Enormous spider webs stretched across the pathways, glistening like chains of silver.

Brother Michael smiled at her. "Are you all right? Where's Simon?"

Her throat tightened. "He's gone to the plane." Her brain refused to function. She peered up at him. "How did you get here?"

"By truck. Left before dawn."

She hadn't even heard him drive up.

"Brought a crew of students with me to dig."

The boys in the truck stared.

"I couldn't have made it into the valley without them," Michael continued. "We had to dig our way through five landslides."

She couldn't think about landslides. All she could think about was Simon. She swallowed hard. "Did Aunt Cecile get my message?"

"Oh course, but you know your aunt. She had to know you were all right."

"Could you take me home, Michael?" she asked, straining not to cry.

"Of course," he said, blinking. "But . . . what about Simon?"

"He'll fly back." Michael must be able to hear the pounding of her heart. "I can't go up in that plane again."

That, at least, was true. "I'll just check my patient, then we can leave."

~*~

Her bedroom was so small she was dizzy from the pacing, but her restless body wouldn't allow her to sit still. She couldn't prowl around downstairs. Aunt Cecile was sure to ask what was wrong and she didn't want to tell her.

Aunt Cecile adored Simon and Lise couldn't bear it if she saw pity on her aunt's face. She pressed her eyes shut. Her only choice was to return to the States as soon as possible. Put as many miles as she could between Simon and herself.

She glanced down at her watch for the umpteenth time. Only seven o'clock. Her aunt and the other Sisters would be leaving any minute to visit the Sisters in Kudjip. Lise sighed. They had asked her to go with them, but she couldn't see herself quietly sipping tea when what she really felt like doing was running as far and as fast as she could.

There. They were going. Her aunt's car spluttered as it moved down the driveway. Now there was no sound at all. No traffic. No rain. No giggling voices of the Vocational School girls.

Lise ached to the bone, pain piercing her chest every time she thought of Simon. And she was cold. She had been cold all day, though the sun had beat down with the same intensity as had the rains the night before. Shivering, she wrapped her arms around herself, desperate to stir some warmth into her skin.

Her body might be numb but her brain was moving at triple speed. Over and over, it played images of Simon. Simon at the controls of his plane, his face exhilarated; Simon with Connor, a warm smile on his lips; and Simon lying next to her, desire in his eyes. No matter how much she tried, she couldn't close down her mind.

She had to leave. And she had to do it now. Before she had a chance to think about it. Before her aunt had a chance to persuade her differently. Before she saw Simon again and fell apart completely.

She began to move before she was even aware she had made her decision. Her bags were in the closet. Easy to pack. Take everything. Within ten minutes, she was ready.

But where could she go tonight? No planes flew at night. Hysterical laughter threatened to erupt. No night runway lights. Impossible country.

Wonderful country.

She loved it almost as much as she loved Simon. A lump formed in her throat. And Connor.

An hotel? Could she stay there? No. Too empty, too alone. Her resolve might weaken and she'd never manage to leave.

Phone Sylvie. Stay the night with her in Mount Hagen.

She lumbered her bags downstairs and made the call.

Sylvie was delighted to have her stay. Just sorry Lise was leaving New Guinea. See her in an hour.

Nothing for it but to leave. She had made her

arrangements, packed her bags. She would borrow the Vocational Center's truck. Park it at Sylvie's. But now the time had come, she realized she couldn't just leave without saying goodbye to her aunt. She would go first to the Sisters in Kudjip and find Aunt Cecile.

Her bags were heavy. She hadn't had to carry them when she had arrived. Too strong to break, a vise wrapped itself around her chest and squeezed. She mustn't think about Simon. It would only slow her, hold her.

Lise opened the front door. The stars were out, close enough to touch, just as Simon had been last night. She pressed her eyelids closed. He had touched her in every way.

Through him, she had learned to have faith in herself again, learned not to blame herself for something that was out of her control. Learned to love again.

But where was her courage to act on that love?
She didn't dare.
You got nothing unless you dared.
Lise dropped her bags on the porch and raised her hand to her opal. The stone warmed in her hand, felt smooth, like the satiny touch of Simon's skin after making love. It seemed to throb, to pulsate with life.

She stood motionless. A life with Simon. She

didn't want any other. The gold chain he had given her felt good around her neck. Unbreakable, he had said, each link stronger than the one before. As her link with Simon could be if only she dared.

If he dared, too.

Her mouth went dry. She couldn't fly out of his life without hearing from his own lips that he didn't love her.

She had to face the truth, no matter what it was. She had the courage to do that now. He had given her that courage.

But she had to hurry. She had to go to him now before she lost her nerve.

Bright lights lit the drive as a car stopped at the gate. Lise glanced behind her. The door was shut, the dogs safely inside. Probably asleep on the kitchen floor where her aunt had left them. They were off duty when they were put in the kitchen.

For one delirious instant, she prayed it was Simon. Impossible prayer: then his Jeep emerged from behind the shield of light.

He leaped from the Jeep and moved swiftly to the bottom step. His eyes radiated light, his scar a vivid slash on his cheek.

He had come for her. She moved down a step, a single step only, but one which held her future.

It seemed impossibly hard to say what she had to say, but she hung on to her courage. The expression in his eyes gave her all the strength she needed.

Then his gaze left hers and he glanced beyond her. For one long, cold minute he stared at her bags.

"Going somewhere?"

"To the airport!"

His gaze shifted back to hers. His face could have been made of marble for all the expression it showed. "I'll drive you," he said, his voice detached now, disinterested.

The glow of hope flickering to life inside her heart sputtered and went out, leaving her cold as winter rain. She didn't know why he had come, but it wasn't to tell her he loved her.

The pain was more awful than she'd imagined. More lonely than solitude. More dreadful than death.

She swallowed, not sure she could speak. "I can drive myself," she whispered.

"Get in," he directed. He brushed past her on the stairs, but left no warmth in his wake. "I'll get your bags."

She had no strength left to protest. Silently, she went down the stairs. Silently, she climbed into the Jeep. Silently, she watched him load her bags.

Silently, her heart broke.

He slammed shut the trunk and climbed in beside her. Between them, the air was brittle.

"Were you planning to leave without saying goodbye?"

Why was he letting her go?

"I couldn't say goodbye." The words cost her everything she had.

He stared straight ahead, his lips pressed together. He put his hand to the ignition and turned the key. The key shook. Or was it his hand that shook?

He gripped the wheel.

No, his hand wasn't shaking.

He drove the Jeep in a wide circle, then headed down the long drive. They were almost to the gate when he slammed his foot on the brake and cursed.

Turning, he gripped her shoulders.

This time she knew he was trembling.

His eyes bored through hers like radar in the night.

She couldn't afford to hope, couldn't afford for him to see her pain, couldn't afford to have love placed before her like a prize, then snatched away again before she could grab it.

"Damn," he swore again and jerked away. He

put his foot on the gas and hauled the wheel to the right.

She shut her eyes as the Jeep leaped over a bump and flew off the driveway into the trees. Branches scratched its sides, scraping down its length with a sound that hurt her ears. With each foot traveled, her resolutions faltered. Where was he taking her? Why was he taking her?

She pried open her eyes. Ahead lay only a faint outline of a path. Shadows rocketed around them as the Jeep bounced and shook, the light from its headlamps skewing off in all directions.

It seemed like forever before they jerked to a halt in the middle of a banana grove. Simon released his foot from the brake and snapped off the ignition. Lise trembled in the sudden silence, filled with a hope she could no more control than the misery. He had stolen her away like a pirate, but did he intend to give her the treasure of his heart?

"We have to talk," he said, pulling her after him across the seat of the Jeep and through the door. They were alone. So alone, they could have been the last two people on the face of the earth. Broad banana leaves closed around the clearing like walls, keeping the world out, keeping her pain in.

Only the sky was open. The stars shone down on them as though they were lovers. They had been lovers once, but not anymore. The moon was there, too, mocking her, laughing at her. A golden tropical moon, made for romance, not despair.

Finally, she met Simon's eyes. He was waiting for her, his jaw moving as though he were wrestling with himself. His eyes were dark and filled with pain, but there was a fierce strength to them, too. She shivered. It was his strength she most feared. And most loved.

"I can't let you go," he said.

"You want your hospital," she acknowledged. "But you can't make me stay." Not if he didn't love her.

"The people need you," he growled. "They need your skills."

Her shoulders slumped. Was this what dying was like? A complete cessation of pain. A world beyond pain. A world filled with nothingness.

He reached for her, his fingers touching her skin lightly, cupping her chin and lifting her face to the light of the moon. Cruel moon, exposing her agony.

His face was in shadow, then he too raised his head. The moon's light transformed him, softened the harsh lines of his face, melted the fear she could see now in his eyes.

She caught her breath.

"I need you." It seemed more difficult for him to say those words than to face the raging Waghi River in full flood.

A lump formed in her throat. Impossible to breathe. Impossible to think. Possible only to feel. A tingling in her fingertips, a sensation in her veins, an explosion in her heart.

"I love you," he said, his words of love as stark as his pain.

"Why did you wait so long to tell me?" she whispered. She resisted the impulse to stroke his hair back from his temple, not sure even now if he meant what he said.

His eyes grew blacker and, for a moment, fear stared out at her, naked and intense. He ran his finger down her cheek. The motion seemed to help. "Because I wanted you—"

"To work in the hospital?"

"—and the last time I wanted something this badly, I lost everything. My wife, my baby—"

She could hear his heart pounding, feel the sweat on his skin.

"—and you made it awfully damned clear you were only here for a visit."

A visit that would last a lifetime now that he

loved her.

"And you didn't seem to like me much."

"Oh, I liked you," she said softly, her heart clenching with remembered pain.

"I couldn't risk you telling me no."

"I thought you liked to take risks?" she murmured. She experienced a powerful desire to be crushed against his chest and held there forever.

"It seemed the biggest one of all. You were right, loving was the risk I feared most."

"When you weren't there this morning—" She trembled, hating to remember, never wanting to fear again.

"You were asleep. I wanted everything to be perfect."

He drew a line down her neck toward her opal. "I knew how important your aunt was to you. I couldn't make love to her only niece without making a proper commitment."

Commitment. Her heart swelled at the word.

He gazed down at her, the tension in his eyes turning to wonder. Then, his lips met hers, drowning her in warmth. He barely pulled away, barely lifted his lips from hers. "I was overwhelmed with love for you," he murmured, the words vibrating against her skin, moving inwards so she believed them.

"Why didn't you say something?"

"I was afraid to, even then." He hugged her against him fervently, then drew far enough away to look at her face. "I was hoping those gypsy eyes of yours had already read my heart."

She gazed into his eyes and found his heart, exposing to her its message of love clear and pure. Past him, in the sky above the banana trees, the full moon rode high, shining upon their love. Joy rocketed her spirit to the moon and beyond, up amongst the stars, where love is eternal.

She raised her hand to Simon's face and smoothed his brow, desperate to erase the frown etched there so deep. Suddenly, nothing was so important as their love for each other. Not fear, not pain, not the taking of risks. To love was a risk. To admit that love was an even greater risk. But the reward was joy.

"I need you, too," she whispered.

A shudder went through him, rocking his body like the wind rocks a tree. But he stood unbowed, unbroken. He pulled her to him once more.

"I know you don't want to stay in New Guinea," he said, his words muffled against her hair.

She pulled away. "Simon, I—"

He laid two fingers across her lips and gently

stroked away her words. "I love you, Dr. Lise Dawson, and I want you to be my wife, no matter what I have to do to convince you, no matter where I have to go." His eyes were steady. They were honest, loving.

"Just telling me you love me is all that I need." All she ever wanted, and more. "I do want to stay," Lise declared, surer of that than she had ever been of anything.

She loved the country, loved Connor, but most of all, she loved this man before her, this strong, adventurous, risk-taking man.

The earth seemed to move. Lise swayed and fell against him. With a long, quavering sigh, she drew in a deep breath.

Simon touched her hair, setting up a trembling in the pit of her stomach that threatened to spill to her lips. His eyes were clear, dark ebony. Eyes she could trust.

Desire swelled within her, starting from her middle and exploding outward until every muscle, every nerve-ending longed to touch and be touched.

His body tensed and she knew, the way a lover knows, the exact moment when tenderness made way for passion. Although it seemed impossible, he pulled her closer and closer, his chest against hers, until they merged, his breath mingling with hers, his heart sharing her beat.

"I want you, Lise," he groaned. "Now and forever."

The breath she drew in didn't begin to fill her lungs.

"I want you too," she began. "All of you." She stared over his head to the sky above. "For as many years as there are stars in the sky."

He swept her into his arms in a motion as timeless as the country, and laid her on the grass in the center of the clearing, away from all pain and away from the world. The night was so still she could hear every chirp of a cricket, every croak of a frog, but the most thrilling sound of all was the rapid thumping of Simon's heart, joined wildly and erratically by her own.

The moon shafted down on them, like a message from the New Guinea Gods that their love was sacred. Their bed of grass was so soft and fragrant, Lise could only imagine it was paradise.

He knelt beside her, staring wonderingly into her eyes. And then he kissed her. Captured her lips, her body, her very soul, in one warm engulfing motion.

The intensity of his kiss and her own response seized her breath and flung it into the night. She couldn't tell whose hand unbuttoned this or unzipped that, but in an instant they were naked.

His hand swept her body, from her shoulder to her waist, then farther, ever farther, to the heart of her womanhood. Her love exploded in a flood of moisture. When Simon felt it, he groaned and rose above her.

The moon hung behind him, a beacon of light lending magic to their love. Tenderness swelled within her until the quickening of her loins made all thought impossible.

Inflamed, her passion soared, like a shooting star in the sky above. Then, like fairy dust from a magical land, it fell back and entered her, ready to spring to life once more with a kiss.

Simon lay on top of her, his warmth infinitely comforting, infinitely exciting. Then, with a final flurry of kisses along her throat to her mouth, he rolled to one side and cradled her in his arms.

"I love you, Lise Dawson." His voice, this time, was as velvety as the night itself.

Joy soared within her, bringing a smile to her lips and a lightness to her body.

"I got you something in Kol." He stroked the hollow between her breasts. "To show you how I felt. It seemed the only way to tell you at the time. Then things went wrong and I never gave it to you."

He stood and went to the Jeep, his skin glowing golden in the light of the moon. He rummaged in the back and removed a soft, linen bag.

"New Guinea custom," he said, laying down beside her once more. He drew forth a shiny, translucent, pearl-like object, about six inches long and shaped like the crescent moon. The beautiful shell shone with an inner light of its own.

"It's a kina shell," he said huskily. "In New Guinea they form part of the bride price." He tied it around her neck, the shell falling warmly where his hand had been but a moment before.

"Will you marry me, Lise?"

The pounding in her heart swelled in intensity until it matched, then surpassed, the passion of the Kundu drum. It was as if an entire orchestra were joyfully creating a song of exultation. She touched the shell, the symbol of his love for her.

"Yes," she said, lifting her lips to his. "Oh, yes."

– THE END –